PUFFIN CANADA

WOUNDED

ERIC WALTERS is the highly acclaimed, bestselling author of over sixty novels for children and young adults. His novels have won the Silver Birch and Red Maple Awards, as well as numerous other prizes, including the White Pine, Snow Willow, Tiny Torgi, Ruth Schwartz, and IODE Violet Downey Book Awards. He has received honours from the Canadian Library Association Book Awards and the Children's Book Centre, and is a recipient of UNESCO's international award for Literature in Service of Tolerance.

To find out more about Eric and his novels, or to arrange for him to speak at your school, visit his website at www.ericwalters.net.

Also by Eric Walters from Penguin Canada

The Bully Boys

The Hydrofoil Mystery

Trapped in Ice

Camp X

Royal Ransom

Run

Camp 30

Elixir

Shattered

Camp X: Fool's Gold

Sketches

The Pole

The Falls

Voyageur

Black and White

Wounded

ERIC WALTERS

PUFFIN
CANADA

PUFFIN CANADA

Published by the Penguin Group

Penguin Group (Canada), 90 Eglinton Avenue East, Suite 700, Toronto,
Ontario, Canada M4P 2Y3 (a division of Pearson Canada Inc.)

Penguin Group (USA) Inc., 375 Hudson Street, New York, New York 10014, U.S.A.
Penguin Books Ltd, 80 Strand, London WC2R 0RL, England
Penguin Ireland, 25 St Stephen's Green, Dublin 2, Ireland (a division of Penguin Books Ltd)
Penguin Group (Australia), 250 Camberwell Road, Camberwell, Victoria 3124, Australia
(a division of Pearson Australia Group Pty Ltd)
Penguin Books India Pvt Ltd, 11 Community Centre, Panchsheel Park,
New Delhi – 110 017, India
Penguin Group (NZ), 67 Apollo Drive, Rosedale, North Shore 0632, New Zealand
(a division of Pearson New Zealand Ltd)
Penguin Books (South Africa) (Pty) Ltd, 24 Sturdee Avenue, Rosebank,
Johannesburg 2196, South Africa

Penguin Books Ltd, Registered Offices: 80 Strand, London WC2R 0RL, England

First published 2009

1 2 3 4 5 6 7 8 9 10 (WEB)

Manufactured in Canada.

Library and Archives Canada Cataloguing in Publication data available upon request to the publisher.

ISBN: 987-0-14-317177-5

Visit the Penguin Group (Canada) website at **www.penguin.ca**

Special and corporate bulk purchase rates available; please see
www.penguin.ca/corporatesales or call 1-800-810-3104, ext. 477 or 474

In war, there are no unwounded soldiers.

JOSE NAROSKY

This book is dedicated to the members of the Armed Forces and their families. They live their lives, prepared to sacrifice, so that we can enjoy the freedoms of our lives.

CHAPTER ONE

I ROLLED OVER and wrapped the pillow tightly around my head—maybe that would block out the sound. I really needed to sleep some more. No good ... I could still hear the dripping.

It had been raining all night. I actually liked the sound of the rain against the roof. What I wasn't so crazy about was the sound of the rain dripping through the roof and landing in the pots and buckets that were arranged on my bedroom floor. Why did it have to be *my* bedroom that leaked? It would have been so much better if it had been Megan's room—after all, she hardly ever slept in there anyway.

My little sister started out in her own bed every night, but by morning she was usually asleep beside our mother in our parents' bedroom. They had a big, king-sized bed, and there certainly was plenty of room, especially with my father gone. I think my mom even liked having Megan there beside her. That left Megan's bed empty. I thought about going and sleeping in her room ... no, no way ... too many unicorns and stuffed animals and rainbow posters. I'd take the rain over the rainbows any time.

The water continued to drip, hitting different buckets with different sounds. It was almost musical—annoying, but musical. I looked over at the clock. It glowed 6:14 in angry red numbers. It was sixteen minutes too early to get up, but there was no way I was going to get back to sleep now. Actually, that clock hardly ever woke me up. I had a strange internal alarm that almost always woke me up five minutes early. My father was the same.

I threw my legs over the side of the bed and climbed out. The floor was cold. It was dark, but there was enough light coming around the curtains to let me slowly creep around the room. I stooped down to check one of the pots. It was almost filled. I picked it up and the water nearly sloshed over the edge. At least I wouldn't have to worry about ruining the carpet. It was so old and worn and ratty that nothing short of setting it on fire would have made any difference. I carried the pot into the bathroom and poured the water into the tub, and the sound of splashing water reminded me that the pot wasn't the only thing that was full.

I set the pot down on the toilet tank and took a leak. Balanced on one foot I leaned over and kicked the door closed. The last thing I wanted was for my sister or mother to walk in on me mid-pee.

Now that I had an empty bladder, I was reminded that I also had an empty stomach. If one was empty, the other had to be filled—the yin and yang of my bodily functions. I went back to the bedroom and replaced the pot on the floor, and no sooner had I set it down than the first drop hit with a metallic ping. A couple of other pots looked close to full—I'd get them later. I padded down the stairs to the kitchen, trying to avoid the steps that made the most noise—no point in waking up anybody else.

I flicked the switch and the overhead bulb lit up. Despite the brightness, the kitchen still looked dingy. The room needed more light. Actually, that room needed more than just light—it needed things like a tap that didn't leak, a countertop that wasn't warped, cupboard doors that would close ... and a paint job wouldn't have hurt, either. The walls were painted a strange shade of green not found in nature. The way the paint was peeling away, it looked as if the walls were trying to reject it.

I turned on the tap and let the water run for a while until it lost its rusty tinge and became clear. I filled up the glass coffee carafe, put some coffee grounds in the filter, poured the water into the top of the coffee maker, and turned it on. The cure for bad sleep, I figured, was coffee—lots and lots and lots of coffee. My mother had started bugging me about drinking too much of the stuff, but I told her that when she tamed her own ten-cup-a-day habit she could talk to me. She stopped hassling me because she needed the caffeine as much as I did.

I sat down at the table and my chair wobbled. It matched the wobble in the table. The floor was so uneven that nothing sat level. The floor needed to be fixed. The *whole house* needed to be fixed. No, scratch that, it was *beyond* repair. This place needed to be torn down and a new one started.

I tried not to complain. It *was* cheap and it *was* on the base. I liked living on the base much better than living outside the fence. I had lots of friends at school who weren't military, but there was something nice about living on the base and not with the civilians. Being part of the military was like being part of a big extended family. You got to know people. Even people you didn't know, you knew. Maybe I didn't like all of them—let's be honest, some of them were jerks—but how was that different from any other family? Besides, living around civilians was kind of awkward. They really couldn't understand what our lives were like. Although, to be fair, I guess we didn't understand their lives either.

There was just something about everybody having something important in common, everybody understanding what you were thinking and what you were going through. How could anybody who didn't have a parent serving overseas know what it felt like for us? For them, Afghanistan was just a hard-to-spell word on the far side of the map. I guess most people knew there was a war going on, but it was different when it was your father or mother over there fighting, defending our country, risking their lives. How could anybody else know what that felt like?

And then, when I thought about what my father was going through, I felt guilty for complaining about where we were living. So what if we had brown water, peeling paint, and a leaky roof? Compared to where he had been living the last eight months, this place was practically a castle. I tried hard not to complain—and really, even if I did, what difference would it make? My mother couldn't change any of this, and I didn't want to make her feel guilty. I knew there was a protocol involved in getting things fixed, and my mother had filled out the paperwork, but nothing moved very fast. Men and material and resources were being used to help efforts overseas, not to make our lives more cushy. And that was only right.

"I smell coffee."

I turned around. My mother was standing in the doorway, wrapped in her dressing gown.

"It's almost ready."

"Then how about I pour us both a cup and get our engines started?"

This was part of our morning routine. I put on the coffee and she poured us each a cup. This had been part of *her* routine for years, except before she'd always shared it with my dad, not me. I'd been filling in for him in a lot of ways lately. "How did you sleep?" she asked.

"Really fantastic. I had a great night's sleep."

"Really?" she questioned.

I looked at her and shook my head slowly. She wasn't supposed to ask that second question. We had an agreement—we'd both lie to each other and pretend we were sleeping well. It was part of a secondary lie—that we weren't worried about Dad.

"I slept as well as I usually do," I said. "When did Megan come into your bed?"

She shook her head. "I don't even notice any more. I'd probably only notice if she *wasn't* there now."

"Are you working today?" I asked.

"I'm off today and Thursday."

"You know, it would be nice if your days off occasionally fell on a Saturday or Sunday, like the rest of the world."

She gave me a questioning look. "Since when did the military ever get weekends off?" she asked.

"The military is one thing. Wal-Mart is another."

"You know, more people work for Wal-Mart than for the military."

"Well, in that case maybe we should send Wal-Mart over to Afghanistan."

My mother laughed. It was a sound I didn't hear all that often these days, so it was almost like a mission for me to get a chuckle out of her.

"Can't you picture it?" I was getting warmed up. "We could send Wal-Mart greeters out in the mountains to track down Osama bin Laden. They'd be equipped with nothing more than their canes and walkers, and they'd be authorized to not only apprehend terrorists but roll back prices."

She laughed again.

"Let's send Wal-Mart senior citizens into battle. You know how the Marines' motto is 'looking for a few good men'? Ours would be 'looking for a few old men … and women.'"

She laughed again.

"We could call it the Wal-Mart Seniors Greeting Brigade, and you could be part of it!"

"Are you calling me a senior citizen?" she asked, trying to sound terribly offended.

"No, I'm talking about *really* old people … even older than you."

"Oh, thanks, Marcus. I was going to start to make breakfast, but now, ancient as I am, I'm not sure I can even remember how to cook. They say the mind is the first thing to go," she joked.

"I thought it was looks first, mind second … and since you look particularly stunning this morning, I know your mind must be in tiptop shape."

She reached across the table and gave my hand a little squeeze. "What would I do without you?"

"You'll never have to find out," I said. "I'm planning on being one of those peculiar guys who never leaves home and lives with his parents … like, *forever.*"

"I think the military might have something to say about that when you join the Forces," she said.

It was a given that I was going to join up—like my father, and like my grandfathers on both sides of the family. I guess that's sort of inevitable when you're named after a famous Roman general, and my name was Marcus Aurelius Campbell. The Marcus part was no problem, but I didn't tell many people my middle name.

"When you're serving, you won't even get to choose the country you're in," she said.

"You're right there, but I've got that all figured out—I'll bring you and Dad with me. After all, I'll need somebody to do my laundry."

"I think I'll leave that job to your wife."

"Wife? I have a wife?" I asked, feigning shock. "When did this happen?"

"It hasn't happened yet, but it will … and I might even know her name."

"Do you?" I questioned.

"Oh, I'm a lot smarter than you think I am."

"Mom, you couldn't *possibly* be smarter than I think you are. So … what's her name?"

"Courtney."

"Could be Courtney. There are lots of Courtneys in this world."

"But not on this base. I was thinking of Courtney O'Hearn."

"And how would you even know that I like Courtney O'Hearn?"

"A little bird told me."

Yeah, a little bird with a big mouth named Megan, I thought. I needed to change the subject, fast. "So, since you're not going to work today, can I use the car?"

"Afraid not."

"But I'm a good driver."

"I'm sure you are, but I think it would be better if you got your driver's licence first."

"Hey, it's not my fault that I'm fifteen. In some countries they let you drive when you're fourteen."

"And in some countries they let you join the military when you're fourteen."

"Sounds like a good plan to me."

"But we're not in one of those countries," she continued. "If it's any consolation, though, if it were up to me I would let you drive. You're a lot more mature than most sixteen-year-olds, and even a whole lot of forty-year-olds I know."

"The question is, was that a compliment, or do you just know a lot of really, really immature forty-year-olds?"

"Maybe a little of both."

Mom got up and started to make breakfast. I didn't need to tell her what I wanted because she already knew. The second part of our routine was cereal, toast, juice, and a boiled egg.

Mom had started working at Wal-Mart soon after Dad left. There were a lot of weekends but generally the hours were pretty flexible, so she could still be home when Megan needed her, and if she couldn't, then I could help out. I knew that money was part of her decision to work. It was only a minimum-wage job, but a military salary isn't the best in the world and the cash she brought in helped. But it was more about having a place to go, something to do that would take her mind off Dad being away. She would have gone completely loony if she'd just sat around the house all day worrying about him.

Besides, Wal-Mart was, in some bizarre way, a happy place to be. It couldn't have been the work itself—stocking shelves and working the cash weren't exactly anyone's idea of fun. Maybe it was the smiley-face logo or the warm wishes from the greeters at the door, but people generally smiled when they worked there. There was almost a cult feeling to it, except instead of a holy book, God, and prophets, it was all about low prices, profits, and crap made in China.

Megan shuffled into the room. She was wearing her dressing gown and carrying her pillow. I couldn't help but smile a little. On the pillow was Megan's painting of Dad's face. It did look a lot like him, but the image was getting smeared and faded after months of being slept on, drooled on, and carried around the house. Dad was definitely a little the worse for wear. She'd painted the pillow not long after Dad left. It was a craft they did in her support group. Each week a bunch of kids her age whose fathers or mothers were serving overseas would get together and talk about things. She seemed to like it.

There was a group for kids my age, too, but I'd never been. I couldn't figure out how talking about it would change him being gone or the danger he was in. Talk was just talk, and I wasn't going to be wasting my breath complaining or crying about something. The secret was to buck up and get down to it.

Megan settled into the seat opposite mine. She put her pillow on the table and laid her head down on it. There was a little waft of aftershave, Dad's aftershave. Each night, right before she went to bed, Megan and Mom spritzed on a little of Dad's favourite. When they'd first started doing that I'd thought it was stupid, not to mention wasteful. Now, with almost a full bottle gone, I didn't think so any more. It really did help her sleep. It somehow made her feel that Dad was close, and safe, and I guess that somehow made her feel safe, too.

A couple of times I'd sprayed on a little of his aftershave myself. Of course, since I wasn't really shaving yet I guess it was technically *before-shave,* but it reminded me of him. If it hadn't been for the fact that I was afraid we'd run out before he got home, I might have done it more often.

I couldn't figure out why Megan always acted so tired. She slept every night, but, of course, only after she settled in with Mom. I wished they'd stop the game of pretending she was going to sleep in her own bed. Why not bunk down for the night in Mom and Dad's bed and be done with it?

After Dad left, Megan started having worse sleep problems than any of us. It wasn't only that she couldn't get to sleep but that sometimes she woke up with terrible nightmares: "Night terrors" is what Mom called them. I didn't understand the difference, but apparently the counsellor at the group where Megan went explained it to my mother. Night terrors were more like nightmares that kept going even after somebody woke up. They were a little freaky, with the screaming and crying and shaking. Megan's eyes would be wide open, staring into space. Even stranger, in the morning she'd have hardly any memory at all of what had happened.

That was before she'd made her pillow. Since then, she'd had the night terrors only once. Maybe I should have made myself a pillow.

"Can we mark off the calendar?" Megan asked.

"Of course," my mother said.

On the wall we had a gigantic calendar. Next to the date in each square there was a more important number—the number of days until Dad's tour of duty was over and he'd come home. Megan walked over to the calendar and took the black marker that was hanging on a string beside it. She put a big, black X through the number 29. Only 28 days left. I could remember when it was 275. That was eight months ago. Eight down, one to go. Or 247 gone, 28 to go. Or about 90 percent gone, 10 percent to go. I figured the numbers out in any and every way I could. Sometimes I could play with them to make the time sound less, shorter, faster. Not always.

I just hoped the numbers wouldn't change again. Most regular soldiers were on six-month tours. They knew when they were going to go and when they were going to come back. But that wasn't the same with Special Forces. Changes happened. In my father's case, six months became nine months. I knew this was because he was a member of Special Forces. Their work was the most challenging—and dangerous—and wasn't on the same schedule as everybody else. He'd said he was pretty sure his deployment wouldn't be extended again, but he couldn't promise us. For Mom's sake, and for Megan's, I hoped he was right. They needed him at home.

"Now there's only 28 days until my birthday," Megan announced.

"Your birthday was two months ago," I pointed out.

"No it wasn't," Megan said.

"Megan, quit being stupid. You turned ten two months ago and—"

"I'm not stupid, you're stupid, and—"

"Both of you stop!" Mom said firmly. She looked directly at me. "We know your sister's birthday is March third. We also know that she's asked that we don't celebrate it until your father comes back."

"We're going to have my birthday party the day he gets back!" Megan insisted.

"Not the day he gets back," my mother said. "Maybe a week later or—"

"Daddy said I could have it the day he came back," Megan said, cutting her off.

"I know what your father told you," my mother said. "But we're going to have to wait and see how he's feeling. He's going to be pretty tired. Don't you want him to rest so that he can enjoy the party as well?"

"I guess so," Megan said reluctantly.

"So it might have to be a few days later ... not more than a week."

Megan nodded her head. "As long as Daddy's there it doesn't matter if it's two weeks later."

"That's my girl. Now, would you like some breakfast?"

She shook her head. "I'll eat at school."

Her school was on the base, and there was a breakfast program there. My school, the high school, was in town. That was a bit different for me, though not the first time I'd gone to school off base. This was my sixth school. After about the fourth new school I'd found it easier. Changing schools was no big deal. Of course it didn't hurt that there were a bunch of us base kids who went there. It made it even better that one of them was Courtney O'Hearn. That reminded me that I had to tell my sister to shut up.

"Do you think Dad will call today?" Megan asked.

"We can only hope," my mother replied.

"What do you think he's doing right now?" Megan asked. That was a game she always liked to play.

"Well, judging from the time of day, he's probably having an afternoon nap."

Up on the wall above the table was a big map of Afghanistan framed by two clocks. One showed the time here, after seven in the morning, and the other showed the time in Kandahar, Afghanistan. I'd put up the second clock when I got tired of converting time and explaining it to Megan. Now she only had to look. It was eight and a half hours later there, so a bit past three-thirty in the afternoon.

"So if I were there I'd be getting ready to come home from school instead of getting ready to go to school," she said.

"Thanks to Dad you would," I said.

"What do you mean?" she asked.

"When the Taliban were in charge in Afghanistan, no girls were allowed to go to school. That's one of the reasons we're there—you know that. And to protect everyone from terrorists, of course."

Lots of people didn't understand that. Our soldiers were over there to support the government and to help supply aid for all sorts of humanitarian reasons, but they were also fighting the terrorists so that we wouldn't have to fight them here at home. Some people didn't see it that way, but that's what my father had told me, and he knew more than those stupid talking heads on the television.

"Do you really think he'll call today?" Megan asked again.

"We can only hope," my mother repeated. "You know how busy he gets."

I wondered how many times today I'd hear that question—how many times I'd think it myself. It had been over two weeks since we'd heard from Dad. No calls or e-mails. That didn't necessarily mean that anything was wrong. This wasn't even the longest time we'd gone without hearing from him. Once it had been almost three weeks. Dad not calling could mean that he was away from computers and telephones, that he was "outside the wire." Instead of being on the base he was out on an assignment, somewhere in the desert, or maybe in the mountains.

I tried not to let it get to me, but I could feel the nervousness building up in Mom. It was like every day without contact she got herself twisted a little bit tighter, the anxiety wrenched up another notch. She tried not to show it, but I could tell. She showed her anxiety in the strangest way—she cleaned. She scrubbed floors, dusted, vacuumed, arranged cupboards, and washed windows. Right now, ours was probably the cleanest, most organized semi-condemned house in the world.

While Dad not calling didn't mean that anything *was* wrong, it did mean that there was more chance of something going wrong. On the base he was surrounded by thousands of soldiers and security wire and gun placements, and he could hide in bunkers or behind prepared fortifications. I knew the Taliban sometimes lobbed mortars and fired rockets that landed on the base, but that wasn't very likely, and even if something bad did happen they had medical facilities and choppers there to evacuate people if they needed to.

Outside the wire, it was just him and maybe a couple of dozen other soldiers, and a few vehicles, and his rifle. And roadside bombs and bullets and the Taliban and Al-Qaeda.

"You'd better get going," my mother said.

I looked at the clock that was set to local time. It was almost eight—the bus would be showing up in less than fifteen minutes. I jumped to my feet and stuffed the last corner of toast into my mouth.

"I'll be home right after school," I said as I grabbed my backpack and ran for the door.

"No rugby practice after school today?" she asked.

"Not today."

"Have a good day!" my mother sang out.

"Yeah, you too ... both of you."

I was partway out when I skidded to a stop. I ran back into the kitchen.

"Forgot my watch," I explained as I took it off the top of the refrigerator and hurried back out.

Carefully, deliberately, I wrapped the watch around my wrist and did up the buckle. It was my father's ... well, technically *his* father's. My grandpa had given it to him when he'd first joined the army. It would be mine when I joined, but for now, with my father away, he'd asked if I could keep it safe for him. It was strange that it was too dangerous for the watch to be in Afghanistan but it was okay for him to be there.

I wound the watch. No batteries. It had to be wound every day, and I did it each morning. It had a white face with Roman numerals to show the hours and minutes and a long second hand sweeping around. You couldn't wind it too tightly—my father had warned me that I could damage the workings if

I did—so I was always careful. But I also had to wind it enough to make sure it ran through the day. Somehow it was important to me that it never stopped ticking. On some strange level it felt like as long as the watch kept ticking my father would keep ticking, too.

CHAPTER TWO

WALKING THROUGH THE BASE on my way to catch the bus, I thought about how we'd been here for less than a year but still it all looked really familiar, like every other military base. There was no garbage on the streets, the lawns were well tended, fences painted, porches orderly, and even those houses on the verge of collapsing were dressed with a fresh coat of paint and tidy flower beds. As well, every base seemed to have the same street names. They were named after big battles or famous generals. This was the second time, on two different bases, that we'd lived on Vimy Ridge Avenue.

I knew a lot of the families who lived in these houses. Not only because of shared activities since we'd arrived here, but because we'd met before on other military bases. You might lose a friend when a parent was reassigned, but then eventually you'd meet up again at the next base, or the next. And the people that I didn't really know, I at least *knew of.* In army terms, we were a big regimental family. You know, like maybe you didn't really know your third cousins, but you did at least know something about them.

Hardly any of the houses were ever locked. There was no need. Nobody would steal from you. There was a code of honour that went without saying. Not that somebody wouldn't come into your house when you weren't there. If a neighbour needed something, they'd knock and if you weren't home, they'd come in anyway and borrow some milk or a cup of sugar. They'd leave a note on the kitchen table telling you what they'd borrowed, and the next day it would be returned.

There were cars in about half the driveways, different types of vehicles—cars and jeeps and SUVs and pickup trucks—but they shared the same vintage. All were older and had seen better days. There wasn't anything new or fancy to be seen. No Mercedes or BMWs here.

When you lived on base there wasn't really much need to have a car anyway. Everything you needed was there, from a grocery store to a recreation centre to your own movie theatre. Besides, it wasn't like most people had a lot of money to throw around. The military paid okay, especially once you rose in the ranks, but most families lived on one income. If you were in the Forces, it would be hard for your partner to build a career when he or she continually had to pick up and move halfway across the country, or out of the country, on a few weeks' notice.

Some people hated moving. I liked it. I liked the new places and new people and new things to see and do. How many kids my age had lived on the Prairies, the East Coast, in Central Canada, and in Germany? I especially liked Germany. And I think all the travelling made us more aware of the world than most kids our age. I certainly knew what was happening in Afghanistan. Most kids didn't have a clue.

I reached the fence that surrounded the base and followed along. It was metal, chain-link, about three metres high and topped with barbed wire. Inside was us—the military. Outside were the civilians—the people we protected. The thing was, they didn't even really seem to know that that was our job. My father was in Afghanistan to protect them, and if he weren't there the wolves would soon be at their doors. My father had told me more than once that being over there was part of stopping the terrorists from coming here. The subway bombings in London, the trains in Spain, even 9/11—if it could happen in those places, it could happen here, too.

I went through the gate and past the unmanned guardhouse. It always struck me as strange. Why bother having a guardhouse if you weren't going to put guards there? With our soldiers in battle in Afghanistan and all the talk about "domestic terrorism," shouldn't those have been manned? A little more security would have been okay. I didn't *really* think that a bunch of terrorists would show up here, but then again, who'd ever thought that the Twin Towers would be attacked?

There were at least two dozen base kids already waiting at the bus stop, kids in grades nine to twelve. I knew them all, and there was at least one I wanted to get to know a lot better. Courtney was standing slightly off to the side, reading a book and listening to her iPod. Casually I walked up to the group, nodding, exchanging greetings, trying to look cool. Actually, I was pretty cool. I was on a couple of teams at school, I dressed okay, and I wasn't the worst-looking thing in the world—I'd had my share of girls interested in me. I sidled up beside Courtney and she gave me a big smile. Good start. She pulled out one of her earbuds. Even better.

"I didn't think you were going to make it," she said.

"I've got plenty of time."

Almost on cue the bus came into view.

"Seconds," I said. "Timing is everything."

We shuffled into line to get on the bus. I followed Courtney down the aisle and she plopped into an empty seat. I hesitated, wondering if I should sit in the vacant seat in front of her or ... no, this was the moment. I dropped down on the seat beside her and accidentally banged into her leg. She squealed slightly and jumped over. Man, I was *so* smooth.

The bus started moving and I tried to regain my composure, but before I could think of something halfway clever to say, Courtney jumped in.

"Are you going to the school dance Friday?" she asked.

"Oh! I'm ... I'm not really much of a school dance guy, actually."

"I was thinking of going," she said.

"Really? Well, I was kind of thinking that I *might* go."

Sure, play hard to get with the prettiest girl in your grade. What was I thinking?

"If you did, then we could go together."

"Together?" Was she asking me out on a date?

"Yeah, you know, we could drive together. My mother could drive us one way and your mother could drive us the other way. I like to make it as easy as I can for my mom ... you know ... because ..."

She let the sentence trail off because she didn't need to finish it. I knew exactly what she meant. Courtney's father was in Afghanistan, too. He had been gone about three months, so he was still at least three months away from coming home.

"My dad called last night," she said.

"That's great."

"It is, but it's strange," she said. "I never really know what to talk about. It's like anything that's happening in my life doesn't seem that important."

"But you know he wants to hear about it," I said. "My father says it makes his life seem more normal to hear what we're doing. Besides, it's not like he can talk much about what he's doing."

"I know. That's *so* frustrating. Military protocol. Everything's classified. Like the Taliban might be listening in on the extension in the other room."

"I heard they could listen in on cellphones," I said.

"Really?"

I nodded. "Yeah, but mainly I think it's because they don't want to worry us by telling us stuff," I added.

"I think not telling worries me even more. My imagination is probably a lot worse than what's really happening," she said.

"I guess so," I said politely, even though I didn't necessarily agree. I'd seen enough on the news to know how terrible it really was—probably the reality was even *worse* than my imagination. People were getting killed all the time, suicide bombers, body parts in the streets, and—

"My father e-mails us every day, but it was so good to hear his voice yesterday. How long has it been since your father called?" she asked.

"Two weeks."

"But you've had e-mails, right?"

"Not for two weeks."

She didn't say anything, but I could see the reaction in her face ... was it worry, or was she upset?

"It's okay. It's been longer before. He's often assigned away from the base."

"My father has contact with us all the time. Sometimes he e-mails two or three times a day. He doesn't go off base very often."

Courtney's father was in the supply and logistics side of the Forces—what they called a *loggie*—and not in an active combat role. He helped coordinate services for the main base in Kandahar. There was always some danger there, but nothing compared to outside the wire. Inside was relatively safe. Outside was dangerous.

"You know my dad's Special Forces, right?"

"You've mentioned that … a couple of times or so."

I felt embarrassed. I was proud of him, but there was a fine line between proud and bragging, and I guess I did go over that line occasionally. Besides, I wasn't really supposed to talk about his assignment—not too much.

"His unit's probably outside the wire more than any other unit over there," I said.

There was that pride again, although it was also mixed with a real feeling of worry, as well.

"I'd hate it if my father did that. I'm worried enough as it is with him just being on the base, and I know how much more risky it is if—" She stopped mid-sentence. I think she heard what she was saying and realized she shouldn't go any further. "I'm sure he's fine."

"He's fine. For sure," I said. "We would have heard if he wasn't."

"So, do you like to dance?" she asked, quickly changing the subject.

"Me? I'm not really much into ... I *can* dance ... you know, if I *have* to."

"Thanks, Marcus. You make it sound like it would be a jail sentence to dance with me."

Oh no ... why was I being such an idiot? Time for some serious damage control. "No, of course not!" I exclaimed. "I'd ... I'd really *like* to dance with you."

"Well, who knows, I might be able to save a dance for you if you come. Maybe even two or three. If you think you can handle that much *punishment*."

"It's not me that'll be punished. I was thinking more about your feet," I said.

"You'd better not step on me! I'm planning on wearing my new heels, and I have this dress that my mother bought me in Toronto and ... but you don't want to talk about clothes."

I wasn't sure how exactly I could answer that question without getting in trouble, or even if it needed to be answered. Better to shut up and cut my losses, I figured. Then I started to think about Friday night. If my mother was working, then I would have to take care of Megan and I wasn't going to be going anywhere. Unless I could convince my mother to get a babysitter. Sure, I could do that. Probably ... maybe.

"What are *you* going to wear?" Courtney asked.

"Wear?" Apparently, we weren't done with the subject of clothes yet.

"Yeah, to the dance."

"I hadn't really thought much about it," I admitted.

There really wasn't much to think about. I had four pairs of shoes—three pairs of running shoes and a pair of black dress shoes that were probably a little bit too small—plus one pair of rubber boots, my winter boots, and a pair of combat boots. I figured the dress shoes won by default. Maybe I could go with my black jeans and a dress shirt and I could borrow one of my father's ties—assuming my mother could tie it for me.

The bus, mercifully, pulled to a stop in front of the school. That was good, because I was pretty well out of conversation. I'd have to start thinking up things I could talk about at the dance. Maybe I could make mental flash cards, sort of like cheat sheets for conversation. Nothing was worse than an awkward silence, especially when you had your arm around a girl and you were holding hands and your palm was all sweaty and—

"I'll see you third period," Courtney said.

"Yeah, third period." I got up to let her by and gestured for her to lead the way.

"What a gentleman!"

"My mother taught me well."

I followed behind her, although the non-gentlemanly part of me was enjoying the view as she walked down the aisle of the bus.

I DROPPED MY BACKPACK in the corner behind the front door. I was always hungry after school ... and before school, and during school. I was pretty well hungry all the time. My mother said I was going through a "growth spurt." I certainly had been growing. In the eight months my father had been gone I'd gained close to twenty pounds and grown almost three inches. I was nearly as tall as him now, and I knew he'd be surprised when I could stand there and look him straight in the eye.

The house was quiet—probably nobody was home.

"Hello!" I called out as I walked into the kitchen. No answer.

I grabbed a box of Cheerios from the cupboard and headed to the computer. I wanted to check my e-mail. I reached in and took a fistful of cereal, and some of the tasty little *O*s escaped and tumbled onto the keyboard. I picked them up and popped them in my mouth. No sense wasting food.

I clicked on the e-mail and it searched for new messages—there were three, and none of them were from my father, just stupid spam trying to sell me prescription drugs.

No e-mail could mean only one thing: He was still outside the wire, still not on the base, still not safe. Of course, he wasn't *completely* safe even when he was on the base, but I knew from the reports on TV and in the newspapers that nobody had ever been killed on the base, so he was probably safer there than anywhere else in the whole country.

I really wanted an e-mail. Not that it would say much, but I would know he was okay. My father's e-mails never really *could* say much, and he certainly didn't tell us much more in the phone calls. It was like I'd told Courtney—he didn't want to worry us. He wanted us to think that he spent his days lying around, bored, trying to stay out of the heat and away from the dust storms. I knew that wasn't all he did. And Courtney was right—not telling made me worry even more. Because I didn't know when he was doing really dangerous things, I had to assume they were happening all the time.

And maybe they were. Dad was no paper-pusher. Special Forces was the most elite unit in the whole military. Lots and lots of soldiers applied, but almost all of them flunked out during training. Only the best—like my dad—got in. Whatever needed to be done, especially anything that was really dangerous, would end up being a job for Dad and the Special Forces guys. It wasn't like he was some desk jockey, spending his days safely behind the wire. He was usually in the middle of the worst of it. And right now might be one of those times … unless …

I clicked on my e-mail again. I knew it had only been a couple of minutes but he could have just gotten back—no, no new messages. I guess that was too much to hope for, but I wasn't going to stop hoping.

CHAPTER THREE

"WHEN IS MOMMY going to be home?" Megan asked.

I looked up from the computer screen. "Didn't I just answer that question fifteen minutes ago?"

She nodded her head.

"And what did I say?"

"In an hour or two."

"Well, now it's an hour or two minus fifteen minutes. It all depends on what sort of cleanup there is at the end of her shift."

"Can I stay up until she gets home?"

"No. Get into your pyjamas. It's time for you to go to bed."

"Can't I stay up a little bit later?" she pleaded. "It's not like I'm going to sleep."

"I can't make you sleep, but I can make you go to bed."

"I wish Mom had got somebody else to babysit me."

"*You* wish?" I exclaimed. "Do you think this is how I wanted to spend my Friday night?"

"You think I wanted to spend it with you either?" she demanded.

"Tell you what, you go and get in your PJs right now and you can stay up another half hour. Okay?"

"Okay."

She rushed off to get changed and I settled back at the computer. I was online with some friends. Where I should have been was at school, at the dance, with Courtney. But thinking about what I was missing didn't change anything. I was here, and that was that.

When Mom asked me to babysit, I *could* have told her I had someplace to go. I know she would have tried to get another sitter. But I didn't. She needed my help, and we needed the money, so here I sat. There'd be other dances. Well, at least one more dance before the end of the year.

I guess I also had to admit—at least to myself—that I was nervous about the whole thing. I really couldn't dance, and while I'd been interested in girls before, I'd never been *this* interested before Courtney.

"So, do you want to play a game?" Megan stood in the doorway in her pyjamas.

"That was fast."

"Do you want to play a game?"

"Not really."

"*Please?*"

I knew that my choice at this point was to listen to her argue and plead and whine at me for half an hour, or simply agree. I wasn't in the mood to fight. Besides, I knew how difficult going to bed was for her. Maybe a game would make it easier. I guess, as well, I knew that it was important for me not to just treat her like my annoying little sister. With my dad gone and my mom so stressed out, it was important for me to step up and be more than just her obnoxious big brother. Now, what game could we play that wouldn't make me crazy with boredom?

"UNO!" MEGAN YELLED as she slapped down her last card.

"Man, I can't win tonight!" I exclaimed as I threw my cards down in disgust—at least pretend-disgust. I had thrown five games in a row after losing the first one for real. It had taken a lot longer than half an hour, but she was enjoying the games. I was enjoying them, too, and what difference did a few minutes make?

"You stink at Uno!" Megan exclaimed gleefully.

"You're a bad winner!" I replied.

"That's better than being a bad loser," she said, taunting me.

"Who are you calling a loser?"

"There's only one person here, so who do you *think* I'm calling a loser?"

"Oh, I see! So that's the thanks I get for letting you stay up longer and playing cards with you? Look out—now you're going to get it!"

I jumped up, and Megan leaped to her feet and started to run away. I chased her around the table, growling and grunting like some kind of scary monster, and then grabbed her and yanked her off her feet! She screamed and yelled as I threw her over my shoulder.

"Sack of potatoes!" I bellowed as I carted her up the stairs. She giggled and laughed and squirmed so much that I thought I might lose my grip on her.

Like a sack of potatoes—that was what my father always said when he carried her upstairs to put her to bed. That was what he'd said to me when I was little and he'd carried *me* the same way, before I got way too big.

I stopped at the door to Megan's room but I didn't go in. Instead I went down the hall to my parents' bedroom. I threw my little sister off my shoulder and onto their big bed, and she almost bounced off the edge.

"This isn't my room," she said.

"You think I don't know that?" I asked. "I just thought that since you end up here every night you might as well start out here. Doesn't that make sense?"

"I guess so. But Mommy likes me to try to sleep in my bed."

"And how is that working out?" I questioned.

She gave me a shy smile.

"She isn't here right now, and I'm in charge. You snuggle in and I'll get you your pillow."

She wriggled under the covers and I went to her room and grabbed the pillow. As I walked back I caught the smell of Dad's aftershave—it did remind me of him. I stopped and looked at the image she'd painted. There was something about the eyes, and definitely something about the moustache, and the crewcut, and that silly little smile that was more a smirk than a grin that was *so* him. I couldn't help but smile—actually it was *his* smirk, one of the things we shared. We also had the same haircut, and I *did* try to walk like him—not that I'd ever admit that to anybody.

I crept down the hall silently. My plan was to run into the room, jump on the bed, and take a swing at her with the pillow. I peeked into the room and—Megan was kneeling at the side of the bed, saying her prayers. I could hear her mumbling but I couldn't make out any of the words. Still, I was pretty sure I knew what she was praying for.

For a split second I had the bizarre thought that since she couldn't see me coming I could give her a really good shot with the pillow—but that would have been so wrong. Not only would she have been mad, but Mom would have killed me when Megan tattled, which she would have done. Besides, there was no sense in getting God mad at us when we really needed Him on our side right now.

"Amen," she said, and got to her feet and climbed into bed.

Last chance to take a good swing at her now—it would have been a typical big-brother kind of thing to do. Instead I decided to stick with the parent role, and I gently handed the pillow to her. She covered her face and took a deep breath, inhaling Dad's smell. Then she tucked it under her head and snuggled into the bed. She looked happy, as though she didn't have a care in the world. That was nice. That was how it was supposed to be. Ten-year-old girls weren't supposed to worry about whether their fathers were going to die. In fact, fifteen-year-old boys weren't supposed to worry about that either.

"Are you going to sing me a song?" Megan asked.

"Do you really want me to sing you a song?"

She shook her head and giggled. Singing wasn't one of my strengths.

"Can you leave the hall light on?" she asked.

"I can leave the bedroom light on if you want."

"Just the hall."

I flicked off the bedroom light. "I'll be downstairs if you need me."

She didn't say anything.

"Good night, Maggot," I teased.

She giggled as I left the room. Maybe it was okay to be the obnoxious big brother sometimes, too.

CHAPTER FOUR

I HEARD A CAR. I knew it was ours. We really needed to do something about that muffler. I looked up at the clocks. One said ten minutes after eleven at night, our time. The other told me it was twenty minutes to eight in the morning in Kandahar. As Mom was coming home, Dad was starting his day. I had no idea what he was doing—I really wished we'd heard from him. I had checked my e-mail twenty minutes before and still no message. I was becoming slightly compulsive. I knew as soon as he returned to base he'd e-mail us straight away, so obviously he was still outside the wire.

I wondered what the temperature was like for him. The day before the high had been 41 degrees Celsius with a bad wind. I checked out the international weather website almost every day.

Maybe he wasn't even outside the wire any more. Maybe he'd *just* got back. I could maybe check the e-mail one more time . . .

I heard the car door slam and I went to the front door to meet my mother.

"Hey, Mom."

"Hey to you, too." She gave me a big hug and I hugged her back.

She looked pretty tired, worn out. And there was an unmistakable odour coming off her clothes.

"You smell like smoke."

She didn't answer right away. She released her grip and gave me a little smile and shrugged.

"Sorry. I only had the one."

"It smells like more than one to me."

"I took my break outside with the other smokers so there was lots of smoke."

"You told me you had your last cigarette yesterday," I said.

"That was my *second*-last cigarette. Now I'll quit. I promise."

"You shouldn't make promises you can't keep."

"You're right. Maybe this is a stupid time to try to quit, anyway. It's not realistic. I should wait until your father gets home—or at least until we hear from him again. I get so anxious, and before I know it I have a cigarette in my hand."

"I like it better when you clean the house like a crazy person."

She laughed. "I cleaned out part of the back room at the store today. It's so hard not to worry about him … especially when we haven't heard from him in so long."

"Probably impossible not to worry until he gets home."

"So that's decided, then. In twenty-three days I'll officially quit smoking … again."

"It'll be twenty-two days in less than an hour."

"I can't wait for him to get back," she said. "It's been so hard on all of us."

"I think it's been the hardest on Megan," I said.

"I think you're right. Is she asleep?"

"No, she went out clubbing with some friends."

"Very funny."

"Don't worry, she's been asleep for more than an hour," I said.

"Maybe I'll go up and check on her," she said, taking off her coat at last and draping it over the back of a chair.

"She's fine. I peeked in on her about fifteen minutes ago."

"Any problem getting her to sleep?"

"Not really. I let her beat me at Uno for a while to soften her up. Then I let her sleep in your bed. It just seemed to make more sense."

"I guess it does." She kicked her shoes off and headed for the kitchen. "I'm going to put the kettle on—would you like a cup of tea? I've got to sit down. My feet are absolutely killing me."

"Sure, a cup of tea would be nice."

I followed her into the kitchen, where she filled the kettle and then put it on the burner. I jumped up to sit on the counter and felt it give slightly under my weight.

"I passed by your school on the way home," she said. "There was a lot of activity, lots of cars and kids."

"School dance."

"And I guess you were stuck here babysitting."

"That's okay, I didn't mind."

"Didn't you want to go?" she asked.

"I'm not much into dancing," I said. I guess that wasn't really a lie.

"Maybe, but you should go to things like that. School dances aren't all about the dancing, you know. I hear there are sometimes *girls* there ... like maybe Courtney?"

If she was fishing for information about my so-called love life, I wasn't biting. I'd had to call Courtney and explain why I wouldn't be stepping on her toes that night, but she seemed to understand. That was one more reason why I liked her so much.

"Maybe I'll go to the next one ... you know, if you don't need me to babysit."

"I'll find another sitter for sure." She reached out and gave my hand a squeeze. "I don't know how I'd manage without your help. You've really taken on so much responsibility."

"Just doing what Dad asked, being the man of the house while he's gone."

"Yeah, well, soon you'll be able to go back to being the teenage boy of the house," she said, easing herself into a kitchen chair.

"Looking forward to it."

"Any word from your father today?"

"You don't think I would have told you?"

"Maybe I should—"

"I checked my e-mail right before you got in. No new messages."

"This is about the longest we've gone without hearing from him," she pointed out.

"I like to think that no news is good news." As in we hadn't been told that he was injured or dead, so that was good. "He's just outside on a mission."

"I know," she said. "I know."

"He's fine." I tried to sound as though I was completely certain, like I had no doubts. But I had more than doubts.

"I know he is. This could be his last mission before he comes home."

"Really?"

"Well, they wouldn't send him out a few days before he was scheduled to fly out."

I didn't answer that. Twenty-two days was more than a few. Besides, he was a soldier—and Special Forces. He'd go where and when they ordered him to go. If something came up the day before he was going to leave, not only would he go on the mission, he wouldn't come home until it was over. And even then, if something else happened and they needed him, he wouldn't be leaving then either.

The kettle started to whistle. I jumped off the counter. "Let me get it."

I took the kettle off the burner and the whistling faded away. I put a bag in the teapot and then poured in the boiling water.

"This has been the longest year of my life," my mother said, wearily.

"He's been away before."

"But never this long, and never like this."

Of course she was right. Afghanistan was different from a training mission, or Germany, or even being stationed in Bosnia as a Peacekeeper. Peacekeepers were killed there, but it wasn't a war, not like Afghanistan. Besides, it wasn't like I could even remember him being gone for that one—I was only three, almost four.

"But he'll be back soon," she said. "And your sister will be able to sleep in her own bed. And I'll stop smoking again. And we'll all be able to stop worrying and we'll go on holidays and everything will be back to the way it's supposed to be. Everything will be all right again."

And I knew what she was saying was true. As soon as Dad got home, it would be all right again.

CHAPTER FIVE

I KNEW THERE HAD TO BE a hockey or basketball game on somewhere—playoffs in both. I quickly flipped through the channels, searching, searching, searching. It was amazing how much garbage there was on TV. So many lame comedies with so few laughs. So many dramas with no plot. So many reality shows and so little reality. I surfed from station to station and—what was that? A few more channels flipped up before I could get back down to what I'd seen.

Some man in a suit was standing beside somebody in a military uniform at a podium, with a big Canadian flag on the wall behind them. My heart skipped a beat. I was scared that I knew what that could mean.

I turned up the volume. I had caught them mid-announcement.

"... with great regret that we come before you to report an incident involving members of the Canadian Forces stationed in Afghanistan."

I was right. I had to fight the urge to change the channel and run from the room. That wouldn't help me. There was no place to hide—whatever had happened had happened. Besides, soon, maybe within a few minutes, the phone calls would start. It might be a relative, or a neighbour, or a friend, or somebody we hardly even knew who had seen the news and would want to ask us if it was Dad.

"I'm going to ask Captain McDonald to tell us about the circumstances," the man in the suit said.

I sat frozen in my seat, eyes glued to the screen, holding my breath, waiting as the civilian in the suit retreated and the captain stepped up to the microphones. There were dozens and dozens of them. He noisily cleared his throat. He looked nervous. I felt terrified.

"At approximately 11 A.M., Eastern Standard Time, which is approximately 7:30 P.M. Kandahar time ..."

"Just tell us what happened," I hissed at the set.

"... members of the Canadian Forces were on patrol when their vehicle hit a roadside IED, an Improvised Explosive Device. There were seven men in the vehicle."

"What sort of vehicle?" I muttered. That would let me know how bad it would be and give me a hint if it was Dad, because I knew what he usually travelled in, a Coyote.

"The bomb was detonated remotely ..." he stated, looking down at a piece of paper.

"Get on with it ... get on with it."

"... and there were four casualties."

Casualties—that was injuries. Even if it was Dad, he was only injured ... but how badly?

"Of those four, only one was injured seriously, and his condition is not, at this time, considered life-threatening."

I finally exhaled. If Dad was one of the injured, then the worst we could expect was that he'd have to be evacuated and would return home sooner than planned.

My mind started playing a stupid game, bargaining with God. If he was injured, and it wasn't that bad, he'd come straight home now, and there was no chance that he would be killed. But if I prayed that he wasn't one of the injured men, then he'd have to stay, and he might get killed before he could make it home. So by praying for him *not* to be one of the injured, I was really praying for him to maybe die, and ... aw, I couldn't do this.

"Two of the soldiers escaped without injuries."

He paused, and I quickly did the math in my head. Four injured and two not injured. That was six. He'd said there were seven in the vehicle. That meant ...

"It is with great regret that I announce that one member of the Canadian Forces was killed in the explosion."

My heart rose right up into my throat. I had to tell my mom. She had to watch this … she had to know. I stood up and—my mother was standing in the doorway. Her hand was covering her mouth and she was pale. She looked as though she was going to faint.

"Mom … there's a soldier who was … who was …"

"I was listening."

"But … is it … is it … have you heard anything … has anybody called you?"

She shook her head. "Turn it up."

I turned up the volume, and Mom sat down on the couch beside me, taking my hand in hers.

"The soldier was a long-standing member of Canada's military who had been stationed in Afghanistan."

Like my father.

"There are hundreds and hundreds of our men in Afghanistan," my mother said, answering my unasked question. "It means nothing."

"We are not releasing the name at this time, pending notification of his next of kin," the captain said.

"So since we haven't heard from them, it isn't Dad, right?"

"They'd contact us."

"And you *haven't* heard, so that means it isn't him?"

She opened her mouth to say something and then didn't. I knew what she was going to say, what was in her mind—they hadn't contacted us *yet*. It could be that the news, beamed across the world by satellite, was moving faster than they could move to tell us. I wanted her to lie to me, but we both knew the truth, and we couldn't lie to each other or pretend.

"Maybe your father is back at the base but because of the casualties he hasn't been able to contact us," my mother said.

As soon as there was a death the entire base, the whole contingent went into communication lock-down, or *comlock.* No e-mail or phone calls allowed in or out until the next of kin had been informed. This was to make sure that nobody accidentally spoke to the family or the media before everyone had been notified formally. That was only fair and respectful. But for everybody else it made it harder. It would have been so much better if my father could have called us to simply say, "It wasn't me." But now, with a death reported, he couldn't contact us at all.

Suddenly the phone rang and I practically jumped straight into the air. I felt my mother tense up beside me. The phone rang again. I sat there, unable to move. I couldn't answer the phone. I *wouldn't* answer the phone.

My mother rose to her feet. Slowly she walked over as it rang a third time. I wanted to scream out at her not to get it. As long as she didn't pick it up, as long as nobody informed us, then my father was fine. She picked it up.

"Hello? ... Oh, hello, Helen," she said.

It was my aunt—her sister. Again, a wave of relief washed over me.

"Yes, we were watching the news," my mother said.

My relief instantly turned to anger. Why didn't these people leave us alone? Did they think that calling us would make us feel better?

"Helen, you know I'd call if I knew anything," my mother said. "No, no, of course I don't mind you calling."

"I do!" I snapped.

My mother shot me a dirty look and gestured for me to be quiet.

"I know you called because you're concerned. We're all concerned."

I walked out of the room before I could say something more that I shouldn't. Besides, I didn't want to hear any more of this end of the conversation. Or any of the other calls that would soon come in. My mother said people called because they were worried, concerned, wanted to support us. But if people really wanted to support us, they'd leave us in peace.

Auntie Helen should have known better. Maybe she was a civilian, but she'd grown up on a military base. But then again, her father, my grandfather, had never been away in a war zone. The only time he'd been assigned outside the country was when he was stationed in Germany. That wasn't exactly

Afghanistan. The biggest danger in Germany was from eating a bad bratwurst.

I turned on the tap and let the cold water run. I put my hands underneath the flow, pretending to wash them. All I really wanted was the coolness of the water against my skin. I splashed my face. It felt good.

"Are you all right?" my mother asked.

"Yeah, fine. Everything is wonderful." I didn't turn around.

"Marcus?"

"Yeah?"

She put an arm around my shoulders and hugged me from behind. I had a sudden urge to brush her away—I didn't want to be touched right now—but I knew she needed the contact.

"We've gone through this a dozen times in the last eight months," she whispered in my ear. "And it's always all right."

I didn't answer her because she was talking to herself at least as much as she was talking to me. Besides, it didn't mean anything. Just because it hadn't been him before didn't mean it wasn't him this time.

"You know your father wouldn't want us to worry about him. We have to have faith that he's—"

The phone rang again and both of us started.

"I'd better get that." She released her grip and I felt the loss of her arms around me. "I wish that was your father," she said as she went for the phone.

"It's not him," I said, stating the obvious.

"He may not even know that there's been a death," she said.

She was right. If he was out on an operation or on patrol he wouldn't hear about it until he returned to base. It always seemed strange that those of us on the other side of the planet could get the news before somebody on the other side of a hill. That had happened more than once. We'd hear about something on TV—an explosion or an operation being announced—and we'd send him an e-mail and it would turn out that he was completely clueless about it.

Slowly she walked toward the phone as it rang for the fifth time. I turned off the tap so I could hear her answer in the other room.

"Hello?" my mother said. She sounded so confident, so optimistic. "Yes … yes, we did hear the news on the TV."

It wasn't anybody official. Only another *caring* call.

At least it wasn't somebody trying to notify us that he was—I stopped myself. We just didn't know. We just couldn't know. All we could do was hope. And pray.

I closed my eyes, bowed my head, and silently began to recite the Lord's Prayer. I was saying a lot of prayers these days—a lot more than before Dad had left.

CHAPTER SIX

I TRIED TO FOCUS on the blackboard, but I couldn't for more than a few seconds, half a minute at the most. I had to hope that none of this was going to count too much on the exam.

My body was in class but my head was thousands and thousands of kilometres away. I was thinking about my father. Where was he, what was he doing, and, most important, was he okay? I'd been awake for a good chunk of the night, worrying, listening to my mother moving around, too—she probably hadn't slept either. And all night I'd felt this awful sense of anticipation, waiting for the phone to ring, or listening for a car to drive up, a knock at the door. I think I heard every car that drove by.

When my alarm had finally gone off, for a split second it had sounded like a phone and I'd almost jumped out of bed to answer it. I was so grateful when I realized it was the clock. No phone call. Nobody had called all night. Nobody had come to the door. We hadn't been *informed,* so maybe there was nothing to be informed about. Maybe.

Funny, though sleep had been out of reach all night, right now I figured if I put my head down on the desk I could drift right off. There was something about Mr. Jones's voice that induced drowsiness. He was like a human cure for insomnia. Maybe I should have painted *his* face on a pillow. And instead of aftershave I could have put chalk dust or the smell of cafeteria food.

I chuckled to myself at the thought but quickly muffled the sound. I had to be careful, because when I was tired I found things really funny—things that weren't normally even remotely amusing. I knew I was in trouble if I started to find *myself* hysterically funny, because, really, I wasn't all *that* funny at the best of times.

The bus ride that morning from the base into school had been louder than usual. Lots of laughter, loud voices, people fooling around. It was almost always that way after a death had been announced. It had happened a few times before I'd noticed the pattern, and I wasn't sure if anybody else was even aware of it. It was all part of that denial thing that people did. If we laughed, then nothing could possibly be wrong. If we smiled, we had to be happy. If we acted like there was nothing to worry about, then obviously there *was* nothing to worry about. Too bad I wasn't able to fool myself that way.

All of the kids on the bus had heard about the injuries and the fatality. There was like a jungle telegraph on the base where everybody knew everything instantly. Like Facebook, except it really was face-to-face, person-to-person. There were very few secrets on a base—well, except that none of us knew the really important information, the names of the people involved.

A lot of the kids—even those with a parent in Afghanistan—were reasonably calm, pretty sure they had nothing much to worry about. Guys working in the motor pool or working in supply—loggies, like Courtney's father—were pretty safe, after all. Courtney didn't seem very worried.

Of course my father was almost always off base. Special Forces men—especially snipers, which is what he was—spent more time outside than anybody else. More time outside meant more time in the danger zones, more time for something to happen, more time to—I closed down my mind. This wasn't helping.

I turned around and stole a glance at Courtney. She was sitting, taking notes. She really was very pretty. Of course we'd sat together on the bus today. Normally she did most of the talking and I did most of the listening. I was following some advice my father had given me. He'd said that girls like a good listener. He'd also told me that the most important phrases in a relationship are "Yes, dear," "I'm sorry, dear," and

"I was wrong." My father lived by the simple creed "Happy wife, happy life."

He was a good husband. He was a good father. He was a good soldier. I knew that it wasn't cool for a fifteen-year-old to look up to his father, but he was kind of like my hero. Scratch that—he *was* my hero. He was over there risking his life for all of us.

Civilians never really seemed to get it. They lived their lives, their safe little lives, doing what they did—working, shopping, playing—and never really thinking about the people who were over there protecting them and their way of life. I guess when they flashed through the news and heard a report or saw a coffin coming back they thought about it for a few seconds. And then they went off to the mall or turned on a TV show or went to bed. And slept. Boy, I'd have loved to sleep ...

"Mr. Jones?" It was a female voice over the P.A. system.

"Yes," he replied, turning to face the intercom.

"Is Marcus Campbell in class?" she asked.

I started into full consciousness.

"Um ..." He looked around the room until his eyes settled on me. "Yes, he is."

"He needs to come to the office," she said.

There were catcalls and *oohs* from the rest of the class.

"You're in trouble now," the boy beside me said jokingly.

I knew I'd done nothing wrong, nothing serious enough to get me sent to the office ... unless ... I sat there, stunned, not able to believe what it could possibly be.

"Marcus," Mr. Jones called out. "Are you waiting for me to carry you to the office?"

A bunch of kids chuckled.

"No, sir."

"Then go!" He pointed to the door.

I stumbled to my feet. I thought for a second about gathering up my things in case I wasn't coming back, but then, if I wasn't coming back, I wouldn't be sweating my math homework. Mr. Jones started teaching again and everybody turned back to face him. Only my base friends had even the vaguest idea what any of this might mean. For civilian kids, it was just a trip to the office. They figured I might be facing a detention, or at worst a suspension. Nobody would die. Nobody *had* died. They couldn't know what I was thinking, what I was going through.

Courtney caught my eye as I walked by. She looked worried and upset and even scared, and that look made me feel even worse. As I passed by she reached out and took my hand. She squeezed it slightly and let it go. There were no words, but I knew what she was saying.

The hall was empty and silent. I stopped and leaned against the lockers. Was this the way I was going to find out? Was my mother waiting for me down there at the office? Would she be standing with a couple of officers and maybe the company chaplain, the Padre? I wondered if my sister would be there, too—or were they going to tell me first so that we could all go together to tell her? How would she deal with it ... how would my mother deal with it? It would be bad enough for me, but having to help them through it would be even worse. I wished I could spare them the pain ... *Shut up! Stop thinking like this!* I ordered myself.

Down the hallway was an exit leading out to the parking lot. I had to fight the urge to make a run for it. If nobody told me, then I could at least live a little bit longer without knowing. I could pretend that everything was all right, because until they told me I wouldn't truly know.

No, I knew I couldn't do that. This wasn't about me. This was about my mother needing me.

Somehow my feet took me to the office, and now there was no turning back. There were half a dozen other students at the counter but nobody else in sight. Not my mother, no military personnel in uniforms, no Padre. Before I could feel relieved, though, it popped into my head that they'd probably be waiting in the principal's or the vice-principal's private office. The school wouldn't have kept them standing around in the main office area. It would be insensitive to give me the bad news out there in front of other students ... about as insensitive as calling somebody down over the P.A.

"Marcus."

I turned around. It was Mrs. Harper, the guidance counsellor.

"They should have called you down to the Guidance department office," she said.

The Guidance department. That made sense. It was quieter, more private. That's where they'd be waiting.

"Come," she said, and I followed behind.

"It certainly is a beautiful spring day," she said.

What was she talking about? Why was she being so cheerful? No, I knew that people did that—pretended, made small talk, laughed for no reason. I still wasn't sure why, though.

There was nobody in the Guidance department except for a secretary sitting at her desk fanning through a magazine. Music played quietly in the background. Mrs. Harper led me into her office—her empty office. Where was everybody?

"These arrived today," she said, holding out some pamphlets.

Dumbly I took them and looked down. They were brochures from the Royal Military College—the place where I wanted to go to university.

"I wanted you to be the first to have them." She had a big, friendly smile on her face.

My head reeled. *This* was why I'd been called down? This had nothing to do with anything about my father. Part of me was so relieved, so happy, that I wanted to scream for joy. But there was another feeling that was building—raw, pure anger. I felt like yelling at her, swearing at her, telling her what an idiot she'd been and how much grief she'd caused me. She didn't have the slightest idea what she'd just put me through and she … she … She really didn't know. It wasn't her fault.

"Marcus, are you all right?"

I came out of my thoughts. "I'm okay … kind of tired."

"Are you having trouble sleeping?"

"A little."

"Lots of kids have sleep problems, especially around mid-terms. You'll do fine, you're a smart kid."

"Thank you. I'd better get back to class." I got to my feet.

"Let me know if there's any more information I can get you."

"Thank you."

"And if there's anything that's bothering you that you want to talk about," she called out, "you know my door is always open."

For a split second that sounded so appealing. There was so much that I wanted to talk about, but no, talking wasn't going to change anything.

I walked down the hall, back toward class. My legs suddenly felt all weak and I put a hand against the lockers to steady myself. My whole body felt hot, and for a second I thought I was going to throw up. I had to find someplace to sit down, and that place wasn't back in class. I didn't want anybody to see me like this. Maybe I could slip outside—a little fresh air could only help.

I pushed through the exit doors and went down the stairs leading to the parking lot. Thank goodness the stairwell was empty. I didn't want to see anybody, especially not anybody that I knew. Outside, I was relieved to see that there was nobody in sight. I slumped down on the grass, my back against the wall of the building. The coolness of both felt good. I couldn't believe how exhausted I was. It was as if I'd just finished running a marathon. At least my stomach had settled.

I took in a deep breath. The air was fresh and felt good. I needed a few minutes to myself to recover from what had happened—or more accurately, what *hadn't* happened. In a few short minutes I'd gone through a whole range of emotions, from worried and tired to scared and terrified, on to relieved and angry and then back again to relieved. Now, sitting here, I wondered how long before the worry would return again. Was Dad really all right? Maybe comlock had been lifted and he *had* called and we didn't know it yet, because Megan and I were at school and Mom was at work. We'd get home and there'd be a message on the answering machine from him and an e-mail on the computer—an e-mail! I could go to the library and check my e-mail! If there was a message, I'd know there was no need to worry any more. Of course, if there was nothing, I'd be even more worried because it would have been another three hours without him contacting us. Regardless, I had to check.

I started to get up when I noticed a car pulling into the parking lot—a military car. I stood there and watched as the back door opened and the Commander and the Padre got out.

CHAPTER SEVEN

THEY COULD BE HERE for only one reason—the same reason that had been twisting my guts from the time I was called down to the office in the first place. I watched them as they walked in the front door and disappeared. I had to get back to class. If they were here for me, I had to be where they'd expect me to be.

I started off and then spun back around. I'd left the college brochures on the grass. I bent down and scooped them up. Then I hurried up the stairs, taking them two and three at a time. The adrenalin of fear had given me strength again.

Quickly I moved down the hall and opened the door to our class. As I entered, Mr. Jones stopped teaching, and everybody turned around to see who it was. Satisfied that it was only me, Mr. Jones went back to his lesson and everybody swung back around to watch him. Everybody except Courtney.

Her eyes followed me as I walked. She looked worried, scared, upset. Her eyes pleaded with me for an answer.

"It was nothing," I whispered. "Just these." I showed her the brochures.

She looked shocked and then relieved, and she smiled.

I slumped down into my seat.

What Courtney didn't know was that she *shouldn't* have felt relieved. She should have felt worried. She, of course, had no idea about the Commander and the Padre arriving. She had no idea, and I couldn't tell her. And even if I could have told her, I wouldn't have. If it had nothing to do with her father, then she didn't need to know. It would only worry her for no reason. And if it was about her father, she'd know soon enough. Being worried for a few extra minutes wasn't going to do her any good. And, of course, the odds were so long against it being her father—loggies hardly ever died.

I did some mental math. There were thirty-eight—no, thirty-nine of us who came in on the bus from the base. There were also others who drove themselves in or got rides because they had a parent who worked in town, at least ten of them. That meant there were almost fifty military kids in the school. And that meant that there was about a two percent chance that this had anything to do with me.

Those were good odds. There was only a one-in-fifty chance that the officers coming here today had anything to do with me.

Wait, that wasn't right. There were fifty military kids, but there couldn't have been more than twenty of us who had a father or mother in Afghanistan right now. Suddenly the odds went up to one in twenty—a five percent chance. Not terrible, but worse than before. And, of course, not all the soldiers were in equal danger. Because my father's job was much more dangerous than almost anybody else's, the risk wasn't five percent. It had to be higher. But how much higher? Was it ... six ... seven ... maybe ten percent? And since we hadn't heard from him in days and days, that made the odds even worse.

Right now, the Commander and the Padre were somewhere in the school. Were they with the principal in his office? Had somebody already been called out of class? Was that person right now walking down the hall—the way I'd just walked down the hall—not knowing why they were being called down, but suspecting the worst?

How long had it been since I'd seen the officers walk into the school? How much time had passed? It had to be five or six ... maybe even ten minutes. Surely if they were going to call me down it would have happened by now. It couldn't take that long to push the P.A. button ... could it? Maybe it would take longer. They might have to make polite conversation and discuss how they were going to do it, how they were going to tell somebody that his world had suddenly shifted out from under him.

I went to look down at my watch and then hesitated, frozen, not looking. What if I looked and the watch wasn't ticking any more? That would mean that he was … he was … no, that would only mean that I was stupid and had forgotten to wind it this morning.

I looked down. The time was right. I held it up to my ear to hear it ticking. I wanted it to keep ticking, because each second without a call increased the odds that it wasn't coming to this class. Somewhere out there, somebody else would have been told the terrible news.

I kept the watch against my ear and I worked hard to drown out the droning of Mr. Jones. The only sound that mattered was the ticking of the watch and the silence of the P.A. If nobody called in the next ten minutes then I'd be safe for sure. All I had to do was count each tick, count to six hundred—ten minutes, six hundred seconds—and it would all be over. Whoever they were here to see wouldn't be me.

I started counting. There was a quiet rhythm to the ticking and the counting as the numbers began to add up. It was almost like a form of meditation. There was a peace. Numbers made sense. I knew which one followed the last. There was an orderliness that chased away the unknowns, the uncontrollables, the unpredictables out of my head and out of my life. The P.A. remained silent as the numbers rolled up. This was one more bullet that I was going to dodge. More important, another bullet that my father *had* dodged.

Then there was a knock on the door.

Mr. Jones kept on teaching. Hadn't he heard? There had been knocking … right? Nobody else seemed to notice. Maybe there *hadn't* been a knock. I kept counting in my head. I just had to get to six hundred and everything would be—the knocking came again, and louder.

Mr. Jones stopped teaching. "Could somebody get that, please?" he called out.

A guy in the back row got up. I held on to the bizarre belief that if I could get to six hundred before he reached the door … no, that didn't make any sense. Besides, I was almost two hundred numbers short.

The door was opened and the Commander and the Padre filled the space. It was my worst nightmare, and it had followed me from the base, up from the office, and right here to my class. This was it. In a few seconds they were going to tell me, and there was no way I could even try to pretend it wasn't true.

And then the Padre shifted to one side and I saw Courtney's mother.

CHAPTER EIGHT

I CAUGHT A GLIMPSE of her face as Courtney stood up, turned, and started to walk toward the door. In that split second I saw such pain and sadness that it almost made me cry out. Just before she reached the door her legs seemed to give out and she staggered, and the Commander reached out and grabbed her by the arm to support her. Her mother wrapped her arms around her and Courtney buried her face in her chest. The Padre ushered them out into the hall, and the door was closed behind them.

And then I could hear Courtney's voice through the door. It was a terrible sound—raw, wounded, piercing. I'd never heard a sound like that before in my life. Everybody in the whole class held their breath and listened. It went on for ten, fifteen, maybe twenty seconds, but it seemed like so much longer. Then the voice faded. Had she been calmed, or had they simply moved away, farther down the hall?

Mr. Jones began to teach again. His voice was the same as it had been a minute before, and he was right back trying to explain the same problem. It was like what had just happened hadn't happened. Hadn't he noticed Courtney leaving the class? Hadn't he heard her scream out in pain? He had to know what this all meant, didn't he? Of course he did, but nobody knew how to deal with it, so he acted as though it hadn't happened. Kids grabbed their pens and started taking notes.

All at once my whole body seemed to melt. All the fear and tension that had been in my back and my shoulders and my jaw drained away. A few short seconds earlier I had been completely positive it was me they were coming for, that they were standing in the doorway waiting to tell me it was my father who had been killed. I was so grateful, I felt so relieved. I said a silent little prayer. *Thank you, God. Thank you.* I had dodged the bullet, my father was alive ... but that bullet had hit Courtney's father, and Courtney.

As suddenly as the relief had washed over me, a wave of guilt overwhelmed me. I looked over at her desk. There was her textbook, and her binder, still open. Her pen had dropped when she got up and was still lying on the floor. Her purse was hanging from the back of her chair. Those were the pieces of evidence that she'd been here only a few seconds before. Her things were here, and she wasn't coming back to get them.

I grabbed my backpack from the floor and stuffed my books inside. Then I got up and went over to Courtney's desk and started to gather her things. I didn't look anywhere except her desk. I knew people were staring at me, and I became aware that Mr. Jones had stopped talking. I looked up at him, standing there at the blackboard. He looked sad, confused, unsure what he was supposed to say.

"I'm going to bring Courtney her things," I said.

"Yes, of course."

I put her books in my bag. I bent down and took the pen and dropped it in as well. I picked up her purse. There was no more room in my backpack so I'd have to carry it. Me, carrying a purse. Somehow now that didn't seem like a very big deal.

"Marcus!" Mr. Jones called out as I went to leave.

I stopped and turned around.

"Please tell her ... tell her family ... how very sorry I am ... how sorry all of us are."

I nodded my head.

I left the class and once again headed down toward the office. What was I going to say when I found her—"Here are your books, here's your purse"?

The halls were still silent, but it was now an eerie silence. Had they brought her to the office or to the Guidance department? No, neither. They weren't going to stay here. They'd get away from the school as soon as possible.

CHAPTER NINE

I WALKED into my room, dropped my things on the floor, and collapsed onto the bed. I felt completely exhausted. The whole day had been like a bad, terrible, scary, out-of-control roller-coaster ride.

After school, all I'd wanted to do was come straight home and give Courtney her stuff, or talk to her, or something, but I had to stay for rugby practice. And in a way that was a good thing, because at least it let me put my mind elsewhere for an hour and a half. I could almost forget about Courtney, and her loss, and my fears about my father, and everything. I was just out there giving and taking hits. It was strange, but when things were going badly elsewhere I actually played better. There was a little more anger in my play. Coach said that was good because he thought I needed to play meaner.

Now that I was home I really wanted to call Courtney to see how she was. Stupid, I know …

I mean, I knew how she *was.* And what was I going to say? But I still had to call ... I had one thing to do first.

I got up and went to my computer. I clicked on the e-mail ... it was receiving mail ... it started to download ... two of seven ... *please not more spam* ... *please just a message from my father.* And there it was! It was my father! I clicked on it.

Hello, Everybody!

I thought I'd drop you all a short note before I go to bed. Sorry I haven't written in so long but I've been outside the wire, and you know what that means—no phones, no Internet, just lots of sand and goats. I've been outside the wire so long that I get thirty-six hours of R and R now—unless something comes up. I'm going to hang around the base and catch up on my sleep. Expect multiple phone calls and e-mails from me. In fact, you'll hear from me so much over the next few days that you'll probably be sick of me bugging you.

Things are really calm here. It was a beautiful day, nice and hot, just the way I love it, and now things are cooling down for the night. My time is getting short here and I'm counting down the days until I can see you. I miss you all so much. I want to hear all about what I've missed since your last e-mail—I want to hear everything. I'm pretty tired so I'm going to turn in. Everything's good. Nobody needs to worry. Marcus, take care of your mother and sister.

Love,
Dad

I took a deep breath. I felt as if a weight had been lifted off my chest, a weight I hadn't even known was there until it was gone. It had been fifteen days since our last contact with Dad, and with each passing day a little bit more weight and worry had been added—then a *lot* more. Now it was … well, *almost* gone.

I grabbed the phone and started to dial my mom's cell number. I stopped myself halfway through. Of course she'd want to know right away, and it would make her feel instantly better, but in those brief seconds when she heard her phone ring and saw it was me she'd be all panicky about why I was calling.

No, it was better that she knew, right now. I started dialling again. The phone clicked and then rang and—

"Hello?"

"He's fine," I said, blurting it out instantly. "He e-mailed and he's fine."

"Your dad is okay," I heard her say. Megan must have been with her. "Thank God, oh, thank God! That's so wonderful!" She sighed, as if she'd been holding her breath for … well, at least fifteen days.

"Thanks for calling me, Marcus … thank you so much. We'll be home soon. Thank you!"

I put the phone down. No sense in wasting daytime minutes. Now we all knew, and we could all rest a little easier. At least for today. Today would be a time for celebration.

And then I thought about Courtney.

Tonight we'd be celebrating, and a few houses away, one street over, Courtney and her mother would be grieving the death of her father—a death that could easily have been ours to suffer.

I got up and went to my bedroom window. I craned my neck so I could look between two houses and catch a glimpse of Courtney's house in the next street over. I couldn't see much of it, but the windows I could see were dark.

I kept feeling guilty all over again. In that rush of relief when I'd realized it wasn't *me* they were coming for—it wasn't *my* father—I had been *glad* it was Courtney. I knew that was wrong ... and it wasn't that I was actually happy that her father had died. I wished it could have been somebody else's dad, not hers. But really, no matter who had been killed, it would have been somebody's father or son or husband. I guess I really wished it could have been someone whose family I didn't know.

Sure, a couple of times when someone had been killed in Afghanistan I'd known *of* the person—two had even lived here on the base. But this was so different. Today I'd been right there. I'd seen Courtney's face, heard the anguish, the pain in her voice. I knew I'd never forget it. It wasn't like any sound I'd ever heard before. The closest I could come to describing it was that it was like the sound a wounded animal would make. But no, it was *so* human—it was maybe the most human sound I'd ever heard. No animal could ever make it because no animal could ever understand loss the same way.

I knew there would be people over at Courtney's house. There would be lots of people coming and going. There'd be counsellors and the volunteers from the MFRC—the Military Family Resource Centre—but there would also be friends, and I guess family members who could drive up right away.

My mother knew Courtney's mom and dad, the way everybody knew everybody, but they weren't really friends. According to some sort of unwritten code, that meant she couldn't go over right away. In a few days she'd appear at their door, probably with a casserole, and offer her condolences. I'd go along then. But I still had Courtney's purse and books. The books didn't matter, but the purse did. She had to be worried about that ... or maybe she hadn't even given it a thought.

I figured I could knock on the door and give the stuff to whoever answered, but I didn't feel right barging in like that. Maybe that was just an excuse, though. If I was being totally honest with myself, I was afraid, not knowing what I was supposed to say, or how I was supposed to act. I'd go tomorrow. For sure.

Talk was already spreading round the base. The body was scheduled to return in two days. There would be a ceremony at the plane when it arrived. There would be soldiers and government officials and family and friends. Then almost immediately it—that was weird ... after someone died ... the body, did it become an "it" instead of a "he"?—well, it, he, would be transported by a convoy of cars to Toronto for the autopsy—like they wouldn't know what had killed him. And from there it would go to where the funeral would take place. I'd heard it was going to be held where Courtney's mother and father were from, in a little town up north. I think it was called Huntsville.

Courtney had told me that her family always spent part of every summer up there, in a cottage that her grandparents owned. She said that when she was little she'd liked it a lot because she got to meet cousins and uncles and aunts that she never saw any other time. But this summer, she'd said, she wasn't looking forward to it the same way. I flattered myself that it had something to do with me, and I guess in a very little way it did. She'd said that she didn't want to leave any of her friends behind because you couldn't afford to waste time. That was one of the things about a military life—you never knew when any summer was going to be your last summer at that base, in that house, with those friends. And even if *you* didn't move, there was no telling if your best friend, or all your friends, were going to be reassigned. Maybe that's why I never really did have a *best* friend. Just friends.

I SAT AT MY DESK working unsuccessfully on my homework. I'd spent a lot more time downloading music than doing schoolwork. I couldn't seem to focus.

We'd talked about the whole thing over supper. We'd even prayed for Courtney's family when we said grace … right after giving thanks for Dad being safe. I'd told my mother I was going to go over with Courtney's things but she'd said that I should wait until tomorrow. I didn't argue. Anyway, I was still trying to figure out exactly what I was going to say.

I came out of my thoughts. I'd heard something … it was like a buzzing. Maybe it was outside … it came again … it was inside the house somewhere. I got up and started across the room and I heard it again, this time *behind* me. It sounded like a cellphone on vibrate, but my phone was downstairs, charging, so it couldn't be mine. And then I realized where it was coming from.

Courtney's purse sat on my bedroom floor where I'd dropped it when I first got home, and the sound was definitely coming from there. I hadn't even thought about what might be in the purse. Was this the first call, or had it been buzzing all night? I picked up the purse and it buzzed and vibrated again. Somebody was calling Courtney. Should I answer it? Should I even go into her purse?

Silently I stood there, holding the purse cautiously as if it were alive, praying that it would simply stop vibrating and I wouldn't have to make a decision. It kept buzzing.

I undid the zipper and carefully, delicately reached in. It felt so wrong, going into somebody's purse without permission, and I was pretty nervous about what else I might find. When the phone buzzed again I plucked it from the bag.

I flipped it open. "Hello?" I said, my voice barely above a whisper.

"Marcus?"

I was stunned. How would anybody know that—?

"It's me … Courtney."

Now I was even more stunned.

"I have your phone," I said, stating the obvious. "Your purse … it was buzzing … I mean your phone. I'm sorry, I didn't mean to go into your purse."

"That's okay, Marcus. When I remembered my purse my mom called the school, and they said someone had brought it home. I thought it was probably you."

"I was going to bring it over tomorrow … I didn't know your phone was in there."

The phone started to beep. I looked at it—it was blinking out a signal that the battery was critically low.

"The battery is almost dead," I said, instantly regretting the words I'd chosen. "We'd better end before the phone goes … before it doesn't work any more. I'll bring you your stuff tomorrow."

The beeping got faster and faster. It wouldn't work for much longer.

"Could you bring it sooner?" she asked.

"Sooner?"

"You could bring it to me now."

"But it's after midnight."

"It's not like I'm going to sleep."

"Do you want me to come to the house?" I asked.

"No, I don't want to risk disturbing my mother. How about if we meet at the park?"

"The park? Sure we can—" I stopped when I realized that the phone was dead and she couldn't hear me. But she had heard me say I was going to meet her, hadn't she? There was only one way to find out.

I picked up the purse and dropped the phone into it, doing up the zipper again. Next I grabbed her books and left my room. There was no light coming from my mother's room. She was probably asleep. I could have woken her and told her where I was going and why I was going there, and she'd have understood, but I didn't really want to wake her.

Hopefully I could be back without her even realizing I'd been gone.

Silently I tiptoed down the stairs. I slipped my shoes on without tying them up and went out through the front door, closing it quietly behind me.

The street was deserted and most of the houses were completely dark. In a few upstairs windows there was a bluish glow, TVs providing the light. The dim street lamps were few and far between and provided almost no light. Softly I padded along the sidewalk toward the little park at the end of Courtney's street. That was the one she'd meant, wasn't it? She couldn't have meant the big park because that was halfway across the base. Either way, I'd try this one first.

I rounded the corner and I could see the outline of the playground equipment—the swings and the slide silhouetted against the sky. I could see the equipment but I couldn't see anybody ... wait ... there was somebody sitting on one of the swings. As I got closer the figure became clearer until I could see that it was a girl. That had to be Courtney. Who else could it be?

She didn't look up as I approached. I stopped right in front of her.

"Hi," I said softly.

She looked up and nodded. Even in the dark I could see the faint lines where tears had run down her face, leaving tracks in her makeup.

"Here." I held out the purse and her books and she took them from me.

"Thanks." She took the phone out and pushed the power button. It came to life for a second and then powered down. The battery had absolutely no charge left.

"I called it half a dozen times," Courtney said. "That's probably what wore down the battery."

"I'm sorry, I wasn't thinking about a phone being in there," I said, "and I really didn't want to go into your purse."

"I forgot about it myself until I started to get calls from friends on the home phone—friends who always call me on my cell. And then I remembered that I'd left it in class when they … when they … when I had to leave."

I could hear the catch in her throat and was afraid that she was going to start to cry. I was even more afraid that I might start to cry as well.

"I was going to bring it around tomorrow," I explained. "I didn't want to disturb you."

"You wouldn't have disturbed me. I'm glad that people called."

Now I felt guilty for not calling.

"But I understand why you didn't," she said. "You were only trying to be thoughtful and considerate of us."

"Yeah," I mumbled. And I hadn't known what to say. I still wasn't sure, but I had to say something. "How's your mom doing?"

"She's asleep now ... well, maybe not asleep, really. The doctor gave her some medication because she couldn't stop crying."

"I guess that was a smart thing to do."

"She needed the pill. She was just ... just ..." She let the sentence trail off. I couldn't imagine my mother being like that.

"He asked me if I wanted some medication, too," Courtney added.

"Did you take it?"

"I took it, but I haven't *taken* it. It's on my night table. If I can't sleep I'll try it."

I was going to point out that it was almost one in the morning and she wasn't sleeping, but I didn't.

"My aunt—my mother's sister—is coming up tomorrow. And my grandparents ... my mother's parents and my father's mother are coming up for the plane arriving."

"That's good."

"My mother needs them to come," she said. "She needs the support."

"It'll be better with them here to help."

"I guess so," she agreed. "You know, when I saw the Commander and the Padre there at the door I knew what it meant, but I couldn't believe it was for me. I thought they were coming for you."

"That's what I thought, too."

"And for that split second before I saw my mother standing behind them, I thought about what I was going to say to you. Somehow I thought it was going to be me trying to console you, and now ..."

I wasn't sure I could say anything that was especially consoling or reassuring.

"You know, you need to try to get some sleep," I said.

"I'm not ready yet. I want to keep thinking about him."

"About your father," I said quietly, feeling instantly stupid—who else would she have been thinking about? "Are you going to take the medication?"

"Maybe later. Right now I don't want to go to sleep. It feels like as long as I'm awake then maybe he's still with us, and once I go to sleep ... then ... then ..." She looked up at me with such sadness in her eyes. "I just can't believe it's all true."

"I understand," I said.

"You do?"

I felt a rush of heat go through my body. Who was I to say that I understood what she was feeling? I had to try to explain.

"It's that when they're away for months at a time it already feels like they're not here anyway. It's not like, he isn't home for supper tonight and that makes it real, because he hasn't been home for supper for months."

"Yeah, that's exactly right," she said, and I felt relieved. "It's all so unreal ... my father can't be gone."

She laughed to herself, and that caught me by surprise.

"'Gone,' that's the word everybody is using the most. Or 'departed,' or 'not with us,' or 'we've lost him.' But he was 'gone' before because he was in Afghanistan. He isn't 'departed' because that means he could return. And he certainly isn't 'lost' because he can't be found!" Courtney sounded angry. "He's dead, that's what he is. He's dead!"

She started sobbing. I didn't know what to say, what to do. Numbly, dumbly, I reached out and put a hand on her shoulder. She lunged forward then and wrapped her arms around me, grabbing me with such force that she practically knocked me backwards. I could feel her body shaking and heaving, feel her tears, wet against my chest, hear her cries so loud in my ears. I didn't know what to say. Maybe I didn't need to say anything. I wrapped my arms around her and just held her.

CHAPTER TEN

I STOOD WELL OFF to the side, partially hidden in the shade provided by one of the buildings. The sun was bright and the sky a brilliant blue without a cloud. It was a beautiful day. That seemed so wrong. It should have been overcast and raining.

From where I stood I could see but was still well away from the passenger terminal—the place where the repatriation ceremony was going to take place … where the family would be. I wanted to see but not be seen. It was a private ceremony, and I really didn't have a right to be there. I just wanted to be there for Courtney—even if she didn't know.

The big Airbus touched down on the runway and I could hear the squeal of the wheels and the roar of the engines as the pilot used reverse thrust to slow it down. It wouldn't be long. That was good, because the waiting was the hardest part.

The day after we'd met in the park, I'd spoken to Courtney on the phone five different times. She'd called me when there were little breaks between people visiting and other things happening. Lots of family had arrived. Some were staying at the Holiday Inn near the base but a lot of people were staying at the O'Hearns' house. I thought it would be good for the house to be filled with people. Somehow all the bustle and commotion might distract them from thinking about who wasn't there. When Courtney found time and space between all the people, she called. She talked and I listened. I didn't really have much to say. I really didn't know what to say, but whatever I *wasn't* saying seemed to be helping. That's what Courtney told me, and she did seem to be doing really well. She was handling it a lot better than I thought I could.

The Airbus taxied toward the terminal. It was a big plane—dark, dark grey, almost black, with markings that were a lighter shade of grey. It was camouflaged to blend into the night sky. The engines roared until it came to a stop beside a shiny black hearse. Off to one side of the terminal sat a half dozen limousines.

Almost immediately a formation of soldiers, all kitted out in dark dress uniforms, came out through the doors of the terminal. They were marching in twos, row after row after row. I tried to count, but there were too many. There had to be at least a hundred of them. If I'd been closer I know I would have recognized most of the men. They marched around the plane and then marshalled up into three ranks facing the hearse and, beyond that, the place where the family would be standing, under a white awning.

Next out of the building was the honour guard—fifteen soldiers with weapons. Right behind them were eight more soldiers. I'd seen enough to know that they were the pallbearers—they'd be carrying the coffin between the plane and the hearse.

Now all that was left was the family. I knew that Captain O'Hearn's parents had come up for the ceremony, along with a brother and sister, some nieces and nephews, and even some cousins. Thank goodness it wasn't only Courtney and her mother. At times like this, family was important.

Almost on cue I saw civilians come out of the terminal building. In the lead were two women—it looked like Courtney and her mother. Two men in uniform followed them. I assumed these were the Commander and the Padre. Behind them were a dozen or more other civilians, men and women and children. Everybody was dressed in solemn, dark colours and they all moved slowly, seriously.

I'd never personally been at one of these ceremonies, but I had seen a couple on TV. It had been strange to watch something on TV that was happening right near my house. Over in the distance I could see the television cameras and press people. They were all clumped together in a little cordoned-off area, close, but not too close, to the family. Courtney had explained to me that, according to military policy, it was the decision of the family as to whether the press could attend or not. She'd told me that at first her mother hadn't wanted them to come, but she'd finally decided that people needed to know what had happened—she felt it was a way for people to know the man they had lost. If it had been us, I wasn't so sure that I'd have let the cameras in. As far as I was concerned, the press were no better than vultures. Live soldiers weren't news. They were here only because there was death. Like vultures, circling a dead animal before they dropped in to feast on it. I was glad they were in that little fenced-in area away from Courtney. Letting them in was one thing. Letting them get close was another.

On my way to the ceremony I'd passed by the main gate. Outside the fence I'd seen hundreds of people standing, waiting for the funeral procession to leave the base. Many of them had been holding little Canadian flags. They were the first of the people who would come out to show their respect. When the hearse and the other vehicles passed by some would salute, others would hold up their flags, and others would stand silently. Again, it was one of those things that I'd seen on the news but never before in person.

Along the highway from the base to Toronto there would be people on all of the overpasses, waiting for the funeral procession to pass underneath. Most would be civilians, but there would also be former soldiers, reserves in uniform, police and firefighters and paramedics, all with the lights of their vehicles flashing. Again, many of them would be carrying flags. This had become a regular practice at each death. The government had even renamed a whole section of Highway 401. It was now called "The Highway of Heroes."

I alternated between thinking that title was completely appropriate and thinking it was wrong. The people who had died had made the ultimate sacrifice, and I guess that did make them heroes, but what about all the other people over there fighting, like my father—weren't they heroes, too? Was it the dying that made you a hero or the fighting? Maybe it was stupid of me to even think that way, but still …

As I watched, the side of the plane opened up to reveal the cargo hold. What a transition: He'd left as a passenger and now he was returning as cargo. That thought sent a shudder throughout my body.

A gigantic ramp rolled toward the aircraft. Two soldiers rode on the ramp and it stopped right beside the plane and then started to rise up until it was level with the opening. I knew what was going to happen next and I held my breath, waiting. Slowly, out of the opening appeared the coffin, draped in the red and white of a Canadian flag. The soldiers eased it out along rollers and onto the elevator ramp. Amidst the dark and drab colours, the red of the flag stood out brightly.

Slowly the elevator lowered the coffin to the tarmac. There was complete silence, as if even the wind that had been gently blowing had stopped. It was so quiet that I could hear the footfalls of the pallbearers. There was a precision to their movements as they lifted the coffin onto their shoulders. Slowly, with small steps, they shuffled forward.

Suddenly a piper began to play—"Amazing Grace." It sent a chill up my spine. It was haunting. It was as much mystical as it was musical. The pallbearers placed the coffin into the hearse and it disappeared from sight. Free of their load, the eight soldiers saluted and then, in tight formation, retreated from the coffin. As they retreated, the family members came forward, led by Courtney and her mother.

Part of me was trying to place myself right there beside Courtney, but I kept fighting those feelings. Showing feelings didn't change them. It wouldn't have made her feel any better, just made me feel worse. And weaker. It was better to be detached, removed, witnessing the whole thing from a safe distance so it wasn't any more real than it had to be. This was as close as I ever wanted to be to a repatriation ceremony. And in a few more days I wouldn't have to worry about any of this any more.

We'd ticked off the calendar this morning: eight more days until my father came home. At least two of those days had to be travel time, and there were three days he'd be debriefing about the mission. They called it decompressing. He'd told us he thought it would be either at the big NATO base in Greece or at a smaller facility in Cyprus. So really he had no more than three or four days on the ground and then he'd be safe. Well, safer.

I remembered reading how people who go on long car trips often crash just before they get home; maybe they relax and lose focus. I didn't want my father to lose focus. No, that wasn't like him. He was one of the most focused people I knew. But then again, there were things that he had no control over. People did die in plane crashes, and it wasn't like he was going to be flying the plane. But right now he was okay. I knew that because a few minutes before I'd left he'd sent another e-mail.

We'd been exchanging a lot of e-mails over the past two days. We talked about all of the usual stuff and a lot about how excited he was that he was coming home—how all of us were excited. But he also wrote about what happened to Courtney's father.

He had been part of the team that had retrieved the vehicle and the body, along with the four wounded men. The Taliban had started a big firefight and it had taken an air strike, artillery, and his Special Forces unit to snuff it out. He said they'd estimated that there were more than fifty terrorists killed. He described the whole scene in more detail than he'd ever written about anything that had happened to him over there. I wasn't sure why he'd done that. Maybe because he knew it was almost over for him.

My father had been there when the body was loaded onto the plane. He'd written to us about the ramp ceremony at his end. We were strangely linked. He had been there when the body was loaded and now I was here when it was unloaded.

He'd also told us some things that I almost wished he hadn't. I knew that there was going to be a closed casket because the body had been too badly damaged, the head almost severed and the face half blown away in the bombing. I knew that, but I knew that Courtney didn't. Hardly anybody knew that. My father had told me and then sworn me to secrecy. I think he had just blurted it all out without thinking and then immediately felt bad about it.

She'd talked to me yesterday about how important it was to set eyes on her father. She'd told me that in some ways she still couldn't believe he was dead, and she wouldn't until then. I knew that even if she did see the body she wouldn't see her father—well, at least she wouldn't see the person she remembered. It would be better if she could hold on to an image of him from when he was alive.

That's what I was going to do—remember him the way I'd last seen him, out front in his parka shovelling the driveway, waving and smiling. He was a nice man, more relaxed and less, well, formal than a lot of the soldiers I knew. A lot of people in the military could take off the uniform but couldn't remove the attitude. Sometimes my father could be like that, especially when he'd been away on training or on assignment. I wondered how long it would take for him to relax when he came back this time. How long it would take for him to let his guard down and stop being a soldier and start being a civilian. It could take a while.

Courtney and her mother walked away from the hearse and were escorted into the back of the first limousine in line. The rest of the people followed and got into the other vehicles. The whole procession started to move slowly across the tarmac. I watched them drive until they rounded the corner of the hangar and disappeared from view. There was nothing else for me to do—or see. I turned and walked away.

CHAPTER ELEVEN

"THIS WAS THE SCENE TODAY, as Captain Ian O'Hearn was laid to rest," the unseen announcer said solemnly.

The camera panned along the road. It was the main street of a little town, stores on either side of the road, and in front of those stores the sidewalks were lined with people, two deep, many of them clutching little Canadian flags. There were so many of those little flags. Somebody was making some money on those—probably somebody who owned a factory in China.

It looked as though every tree and street light also had a big yellow ribbon tied around it. Down the middle of the street came the coffin. It was draped in the Canadian flag and was sitting on a gun carriage, pulled by two horses. Walking alongside was the honour guard—eight soldiers in full dress uniform—followed by four pipers. I was really starting to hate bagpipe music. The same way ginger ale reminded me of being sick, bagpipes now reminded me of death. Behind the pipers was a line of cars. I had to assume that Courtney and her mother were in that first limousine.

"It's been an unseasonably warm day and the sky above was blue and cloudless," the announcer said. "The weather was in contrast to the solemn nature of the occasion as over a thousand people lined the streets of Huntsville today. The church was filled to overflow, with those unable to be in the church watching from the courtyard, where a closed-circuit television broadcast the service."

The scene showed the courtyard, filled with people. They all looked solemn and serious, but many were dressed in clothes that were more suited for the beach than a funeral—lots of blue jeans, casual shirts, and even shorts.

The scene changed to the church and the minister standing at the altar.

"Ian's roots are deep in our community. It was in this church that his parents were married, that he was baptized, that he and his wife were married, and that his daughter was also baptized."

Instantly the screen changed to show Courtney and her mother sitting in the front pew. She sat between her mother and an older man—was that her grandfather? You could tell that all three of them were crying. It was so painful to watch that I almost turned away, but before I could, the image of the minister appeared again.

"Ian was somebody who always tried to do the right thing. There's hardly a person in town who wouldn't have a memory to share. Ian as a boy, swimming in the lake, delivering the paper, cutting grass in the summer or shovelling snow in the winter to earn money, a stand-out defenceman on the local hockey teams. He grew up doing what Canadians do, grew up to be what we are so proud of, a man of high standards and values.

"And the way he grew, and the way he lived, is how he died. He was trying to do the right thing. He was a proud Canadian who gave his life to protect the values that define our country. It was a sacrifice he was willing to make."

But what about the sacrifice of his family? I thought. Were they willing to give up their husband, their father, their uncle, their son? What about them?

There was now an announcer, in a dark suit, microphone in hand, standing on the street with the church behind him.

"Captain O'Hearn was killed by an improvised explosive device, an IED, which was detonated remotely as his vehicle passed over it. He was the eighty-third Canadian fatality in Afghanistan."

The view of the reporter gave way to a photo of Captain O'Hearn. He was in uniform, beret on his head, standing straight, eyes bright, with a Canadian flag off to one side.

"Three other soldiers with him in the vehicle were injured," the announcer said. "One remains in critical condition and has been transported to Germany for further treatment. The question we must pose today is this: How many more of our sons, and daughters, will die in this war, and ultimately, will their sacrifice be worth it?" The reporter paused for dramatic effect. "Reporting from Huntsville, Ontario, this is Cameron Smith."

Back to the newsroom, where two people—a man and a woman—sat behind a desk.

"That is a tragic story," the male reporter said solemnly.

"Yes, tragic," the anchorwoman replied.

They both nodded their heads slowly. She looked as though she was going to cry.

"We're going to a short commercial break," the man said, "and then we'll be back with a story that's guaranteed to put a smile on your face."

Suddenly the woman *was* smiling and—the phone rang.

I jumped up off the couch and did a quick mental calculation as I ran for the phone. It was a little after six here so it would be … too late for this to be my father on the other end of the line. I grabbed the phone.

"Hello?"

"Hi, Marcus, it's me."

"Courtney … but I was—" I stopped myself. Of course, what I was watching was a tape of the funeral and not a live broadcast.

"We just got back from the cemetery."

"How was it?" That was a stupid question, but I couldn't think what else to ask.

"I guess it was as good as it could be. There were lots of people."

"I saw."

"You saw … but …"

"On TV, the news. It was on the news."

"Of course. There were cameras all over the place. Listen, Marcus, I was calling to ask you for a favour."

"You name it," I said.

"I'm not going to be coming back for a while, maybe a week or even two, and I was wondering if you could take notes for me in History."

"Of course. Do you want me to try to find somebody to do the same in your other classes?" I asked.

"Thanks, but I think I can get it covered. I'll call some other people. I'll call you back if I can't."

"Sure, no problem, let me know. Is there anything else I can do? Do you want me to take in the mail or something?"

"If you *could* take in the mail that would be great, and do you think you could water the plants? There aren't many, but there's a couple in the kitchen and one up in my room and one in my parents' room."

"Is it okay for me to go into your house?"

"Well, sure, that's where the plants are. The back door is open. I don't think we even have a key for the lock. That would be so nice, if you could do that."

"I can do it."

"Just once or twice, that's all. I'll call when I know more about how long we're going to be."

"Okay, sure."

"And Marcus, thanks for being there, it means so much to me. Bye-bye."

"Yeah, bye."

I put the phone down. I could water some plants. I could take in the mail. I could take notes in History and give them to her. What I couldn't do was anything that really mattered.

CHAPTER TWELVE

"IS THAT HIM? Is that Daddy?" Megan exclaimed.

"I'm not sure, but I'm hoping," Mom said.

The plane made a lazy turn as it circled the airfield to come in for a landing. It looked identical to the Airbus that had brought back Courtney's father. Maybe it was even the same plane—delivering different news. I hoped it was carrying my father. I looked at my watch. It was the right time. I knew it must have been his, but until it landed, until he got off, until I saw his face and shook his hand, I wasn't prepared to completely believe it.

We'd gotten up early. Really, really early. None of us could get to sleep the night before. That wasn't unusual in itself, but it was for such a different reason now. Not worry or anxiety or upset or concern—it was about anticipation and excitement. The closest thing I could compare it to was the night before Christmas when I was a kid, except this was better, and we were sharing it with other people. There were ten soldiers coming home today and there were at least a hundred people waiting. Wives and kids and parents and girlfriends and assorted other relatives and friends were waiting beside the tarmac, behind a metal barricade—waiting for their loved ones to come off the plane.

On the other side, on the tarmac, stood the honour guard and the base band. Beside them was a little elevated stage that held the Commander, a few of the highest-ranking officers, and a bunch of civilians. I didn't know who they were for sure but I guessed they were mainly politicians and government types. They seemed to like to be here for the homecomings. It somehow seemed wrong that they were allowed closer than the family members. How was that right—that strangers got to greet the soldiers first?

I noticed the area that had held reporters and cameramen for the repatriation ceremony was almost empty now. There were only a couple of them left. I guess life wasn't as exciting as death. They really were vultures ... or was it the public? Did people only want to see death, and the reporters only covered what people wanted to see?

My stomach was starting to grumble. I guess I was a little bit nervous, but mainly hungry. Breakfast had been a long time ago, and we'd been so busy cleaning the house that we'd all sort of forgotten about lunch. We'd been so busy, in fact, that we'd forgotten our usual morning ritual—nobody had crossed off the last day on the calendar. Just before leaving we'd noticed and let Megan "X" out that last day. I couldn't help having stupid thoughts about that part of our routine—like, if we'd left the house without doing that he wouldn't have come home today. His plane would have been delayed. Or, instead of sending him home, he had to go back for one more assignment.

It was stupid to think that not marking the calendar could have that effect, but I'd often had those thoughts since he'd been gone. Like keeping the watch wound—it was all some weird part of magical thinking. It was like I couldn't control what was happening to him but we *could* mark off the days, I *could* keep the watch from running down. And by doing those things, somehow, I could keep him safe. But that all ended today. He was coming home. Now. Appearing before my eyes like a magic trick—"there he wasn't—here he is!"

Dad had called us late the night before from Germany. That was his last stopover on the way home. He sounded about as excited as we felt. He told us he hadn't slept for almost twenty-four hours and that he hoped we didn't mind if he climbed into bed and slept for two days straight. As long as he was *home,* and in *his* bed, in *our* house, he could sleep for the next week. All I wanted was to be able to peek in and see him in bed, and hear him snoring. I never thought I'd be grateful to hear him snoring. Now, it would be like a lullaby!

The plane started to descend, lower and slower, getting bigger and bigger as it came down from the sky. I held my breath as the wheels touched down, and the plane bounced slightly back into the air and then settled onto the ground. A cheer went up from the crowd. The engines roared as the reverse thrust kicked in to slow it down. It came closer and closer, and then rolled on down the runway, passing us where we stood. In those few seconds I tried to look into the cabin windows, hoping to catch a glimpse of Dad, but of course I couldn't see anybody. I imagined he was inside doing the same. The plane continued down the runway, and it almost seemed like one final, cruel joke—to have him come this close and then leave again, even for a few hundred metres and a few minutes.

The plane came almost to a stop and then did a tight circle at the end of the runway and started slowly back toward us. It came to a stop almost right in front of us. We were separated from Dad by a slice of tarmac, an honour guard, and a low metal barricade. The door to the plane would soon open and he'd appear ... soon ... in seconds!

A sudden, surprising silence gripped the crowd. It was as if we were all collectively holding our breath in anticipation. Then all at once the ramp door started to open, the band began to play, and the whole crowd burst into screams and applause.

The first soldier started down the ramp and the cheering got louder—was it Dad? No, too small, wrong rank. Right behind him was another soldier, again, not him, and then a third and—there he was!

"I see him!" I screamed.

"Where, where is he?" Megan demanded. She sounded almost frantic.

I swept her up in my arms. "There he is!"

"I see him too! I see him too!" she shrieked.

The ten men marched across the tarmac, walking between the ranks of the honour guard to exchange first salutes and then handshakes with the Commander. They proceeded to take up positions in a straight line, facing the stage, with their backs to us.

My mother wrapped her arms around both Megan and me. She was fighting hard not to cry but I could see the tears starting to well up in her eyes. Megan wasn't far behind. I knew I had to hold the tears back—there was no way I could let anybody see me cry. I wasn't a woman or a girl or a baby.

The men snapped to attention in response to a command we couldn't hear and the cheering and music instantly stopped, leaving us all in silence except for the sound of clicking cameras.

"At *ease!*" came an order, and the ten men responded.

I took a deep breath, fighting back the emotions I was feeling. It would only be a minute or two at most and—there was the sound of static and I looked up to the stage. Some civilian I didn't recognize was standing at the podium in front of the microphone. He was going to give a speech. I'd forgotten about speeches. Why did anybody have to say anything? And was it going to be just him or were all those people up on stage going to have to say something, too? How long was this going to take?

"Good afternoon," the man began. "On behalf of the Defence Department and the Canadian Government it is my great pleasure to welcome home our brave soldiers!"

The crowd all around me erupted in cheers and screams and applause, including Megan, who hooted and hollered right in my ear so loudly that I jumped. I didn't cheer. I didn't want anybody to give any speech. I wanted them to dismiss the men—dismiss my father—and let us be together again as a family. Wasn't nine months apart enough without another thirty minutes or an hour or … what an idiot … what right did I have to complain? How much would Courtney give to be here waiting for her father, being able to see him across the tarmac. I could wait. Maybe I'd even cheer a little … when it was all over.

He kept on talking, and I kept standing there, holding Megan, my mother's arms around us, staring at my father. Well, at least, at the back of his head. That *was* his head I was staring at, wasn't it? From this distance, from the back, with all the soldiers in uniforms, each wearing a red beret, it was almost impossible to tell them apart. It did look like him, though—about the right height, solid, strong, standing motionless. If only he'd turn around, or even look to the side, for a split second, then I could be certain. But I knew if it was my father, he would never do that. A good soldier always had eyes front, and he was a good soldier. Maybe that's how I could be certain it was my father, because he *didn't* turn around.

I could stare at him for the next hour if necessary. The next two. The next ten. All that mattered was that he was here, safe, and soon we'd all be home together, and everything was going to be all right again.

I started to get stuck in that magical thinking again. As long as I didn't look away from him, as long as I didn't even blink, he'd stay with us. Take my eyes off him for even an instant, though, and maybe he wouldn't be there any more. I couldn't let those thoughts hold me. I lowered my eyes to the ground, closed them for a few seconds, and then looked back. He was still there. I could wait.

There was a round of applause and I was jolted back to reality.

The Commander came up to the microphone. Maybe he'd be the last speaker.

"It is with great pleasure that I will bring this ceremony to a conclusion," the Commander began.

I almost cheered but caught myself in time.

"These men are heroes," he said, gesturing to the soldiers before him. "But they are much more than that. They are sons and brothers, husbands and fathers. And today I am not only proud, but so … *so* happy to be welcoming them home … home to their families." He paused and smiled. "And that ends our ceremony. You are all dismissed."

The crowd began to cheer and clap and the band began to play the Regimental March as the men dispersed. I let my sister down and she and my mother, hand in hand, ran along as the crowd surged through the opening in the barricade and onto the tarmac. I followed slowly behind as they raced, weaving through the crowd toward my father. I knew I should be running to him as well, but I just wanted to watch. For the last nine months I'd been watching them, been the man of the house, made sure they were taken care of.

Megan leaped into Dad's arms, and my mother rushed over and wrapped her arms around him. I smiled. It was his turn again to watch over them. Now I could join them.

My father gazed all around, looking for me. Our eyes met. I brought my hand up and offered a salute.

He broke into a wide grin and saluted me back. I walked over then and offered my hand. He reached out and we shook hands, and then suddenly he pulled me closer and wrapped his arms around me and we hugged. He was finally home. And, despite everything, I started to cry.

CHAPTER THIRTEEN

I ROLLED OVER and looked at the clock. It was almost six-thirty, and as usual my internal clock had woken me up just before the alarm could. I stretched, reached over, and turned off the alarm. Something smelled good. I guessed Mom was up and making breakfast ... and then it all came back in a rush. It could be Mom ... or it could be Dad! He was home!

I jumped out of bed. Again I felt that Christmas-morning rush of excitement. I stomped down the stairs and stopped at the doorway leading into the kitchen. My father was standing at the counter, his back to me, wearing his slippers and some old sweats. He was flipping pancakes on the griddle and humming some tune, but it was so off-key and mumbled that I couldn't even imagine what it was. I'd inherited my father's tone-deafness.

"I'm assuming that either my son or a herd of elephants just came down the stairs," he said without turning around.

"Not much difference."

"There's a big difference." He turned around and gave me a big smirky smile. "I don't hug elephants. Come here!"

I met him halfway and he hugged me, long and so hard that it almost squished the air right out of my lungs.

"I can't get over how big you are," he said, shaking his head.

"I've grown for sure, but I think you've shrunk a little … a sure sign of old age."

He laughed. "Getting older is better than the alternative."

"What's the alternative?" I asked.

"Getting deader." He paused. "Sorry, bad joke … lots of bad jokes where I've been … sort of our way of dealing with things. But really, I have shrunk. I lost almost twenty pounds. Didn't you notice?"

I looked at him closely. He did seem lighter, slimmer, but his arms were still ripped. I was almost his height now but I sure as heck wouldn't have wanted to fight him. I could still feel his hug in my ribs.

"It's hard to maintain your weight over there. The heat melts it off you. It's like living in a sauna."

"I can't even imagine."

"Yeah, I was there, and there are still parts I can't believe are real. The heat and the dust are incredible."

"Sounds more like hell than a sauna."

"Some of it, but it's strange—one minute you're going over ground that looks like you could be on the moon, and a few minutes later you arrive at the gates to the Garden of Eden. There are grapevines, and lush fields, marijuana plants as high as you can reach—"

"Marijuana? Is that legal there?"

"Lots of things are legal ... or at least not illegal, if that makes any sense. Marijuana and hash are pretty common, not to mention the fields filled with opium poppies. And around the fields are low mud walls and buildings and houses two and three storeys tall, and they're all chunked together like some gigantic jigsaw puzzle."

"That does sound kind of pretty."

"And pretty dangerous. Afghanistan's a country that's been at war since the dawn of time, and each of those houses has gun ports and lots of little hiding places. You never know who's watching you, but you can be pretty certain that somebody *is* watching, all the time."

"Makes it sound like you're safer out in the rocks."

"You're right about that. I like to see what's coming at me. Of course, that means they can see you coming, too, the better to either get out of your way or get into your way. But it's still better than being trapped on those narrow little roads between the mud walls and buildings." He paused. "That's where the Taliban likes to fight, hidden among the ordinary villagers."

"I guess they're too chicken to face you out in the open."

He shook his head. "Those people are lots of things, but cowardly isn't one of them."

"Then what would you call them?"

"Smart, brave, ruthless, uncaring for life, whether it's ours, theirs, or even the lives of their people. They don't seem to care if civilians die, even children. That's one of the reasons I don't like fighting them in the villages. We make mistakes—everybody does in the heat of battle—but we'd never target civilians or use them for shields. They would. They don't care if people die, if crops are destroyed, or buildings get blown up."

"The villagers must hate them."

"Some do and some don't. Some are loyal to the Taliban even when they're pretending that they're on our side."

"So they're like spies or traitors?"

"Depends on your point of view. Some people would say that anyone who supports *us* is a traitor or spy. Allegiances and alliances change pretty fast over there. I heard somebody say you can't buy an Afghan, you can only rent him, and as soon as somebody else offers him more money he changes sides."

"Do you believe that?" I asked.

"There's at least some truth to that, and in a way you can't blame them. Some people there, like the religious extremists in the Taliban, they have strong beliefs and definite ideas about which side they're on and who should win. But a lot of the ordinary people are just trying to stay alive and keep food on the table for their families. They've learned that the best way to do that is to go with the flow and try to back a winner. Alexander the Great, Genghis Khan, the British, the Russian, the Americans, and now NATO forces—this is a country that has had to put up with invaders since the dawn of time."

"But we're not invaders—we're there to do good!" I argued.

"Well, again, it all depends on your point of view. Giving women and girls rights, building schools, setting up health clinics—we believe that these are good things. And most of the ordinary folks—the regular Joes, or I guess Mohammads—what most of them want is a roof over their heads, food in their stomachs, clean water to drink, a school for their kids to attend, and a way to earn a living. They're really friendly to us—it's part of their culture to show hospitality, and they'll take in strangers, offer them food and shelter and protection. We've been treating the people a lot better than they were treated by the Taliban, and a lot more fairly than their own police and soldiers treat them. I think when they see a Canadian they expect to be treated fairly."

"And that's why they're shooting at us?"

"That's the extremists, the Taliban and the people who support them. They see what we're doing as wrong. We're interfering with their beliefs, their culture, and to them that's evil. We're trying to do what *we* think is right, but to a lot of people, because we're not Muslims and we don't believe what they believe, we're infidels, and eventually they figure we'll leave on our own or be kicked out."

"Come on, they're not strong enough to kick us out."

"Don't ever underestimate the determination of these people, Marcus. Afghanistan is an easy country to take, but a hard one to hold. Only time will tell."

He'd been talking so fast and with such animation that he hardly seemed like my father. He was usually a man of few words, and this was a pretty heavy conversation to be having before breakfast. Almost on cue then, as if he'd been reading my thoughts, he stopped talking. His eyes were wide open, staring into the distance, seeing something that I couldn't see, something I couldn't even imagine.

"Are you expecting company?" I asked, finally breaking the uneasy silence.

"I hope not. Why?"

"You made enough pancakes for a whole battalion."

"I'm hungry!"

"It looks like you're planning on gaining back the whole twenty pounds you lost before lunch."

"I've made everybody their favourites."

On the counter were two plates, piled high with pancakes. On one plate were chocolate chip pancakes—the favourite of my father and my sister. On the other were the ones made with strawberries and bananas—the pancake of choice for my mother and me.

"Why don't you go and wake up our two Sleeping Beauties?" my father said.

I shook my head. "I think they'd really rather have you wake them up."

"Okay, I'll do that. You take care of the pancakes."

"Deal."

He handed me the flipper, saluted me, and left the room. As he left, he began whistling. His whistling was about as bad as his singing. He stomped up the stairs with the same gentleness I'd used to come down. I didn't care. He could stomp, sing, whistle, and do pretty well anything he wanted. It was just so good to hear him, to know that he was home.

The pancakes were all starting to bubble. I worked the flipper, turning them over, one by one, to reveal a golden-brown side. They all looked perfect. On the counter beside the two filled plates was a big bowl with more batter. How many pancakes did he think the four of us could eat?

I could hear him upstairs—my father didn't really have what you'd call an "indoor voice." I could hear my sister shrieking with joy, and my mother laughing, and as I stood there, watching the pancakes finish cooking,

I felt so happy. Happier than I remembered feeling for a long time. Maybe happier than I'd ever felt.

I carried the pancakes over to the table and noticed then that it was already set, not with the usual jumbled collection of chipped and old dishes but with the good plates and the fancy placemats. The sterling silver was out—my grandmother's—and there were crystal glasses filled with orange juice. There was also a crystal bowl filled with fruit salad and a sterling-silver platter covered with bacon—how had I missed that smell? In the very centre of the arrangement was a vase filled with lilacs. Where had he gotten lilacs? I put the plates down on either side of the vase.

"My goodness!" my mother exclaimed as she entered the kitchen. She was closely followed by my father, carrying Megan on his back. "This is amazing!" She beamed.

"This is how I imagined our first breakfast at home together. Please, everybody, take a seat," my father said.

My father reached around and spun Megan off his back, hugging her, giving her a big sloppy kiss on the forehead, and then plopping her down on her feet.

"Everybody sit down and I'll serve you," my father said. He pulled out a chair and motioned for my mother to sit.

"Thank you," she said, obviously pleased with all the extra attention.

Megan and I sat down as well. My father looked at me then and raised one eyebrow. Suddenly I realized what he was thinking. All the time he'd been gone I'd been sitting in *his* place at the head of the table.

"Sorry, Dad, I kinda got into the habit of—"

He placed a hand on my shoulder to stop me as I started to get up. "No, stay right there. It doesn't matter where I sit at this table as long as I get to sit at this table."

I eased back in but I still felt uncomfortable.

"I was also thinking that something else that started as a temporary arrangement should become permanent now." He paused. "That watch you're wearing."

"But it's your watch!" I protested. "I should have given it back to you right away, but I sort of forgot and—"

"It's the family watch. I never did wear it that much, and it looks pretty good right there on your wrist," he said.

"But it's *your* watch, so you really—"

"No," he said, cutting me off again. "Since it *is* my watch, then *I* should be able to decide what should be done with it. It is now, officially and permanently, *your* watch." He bowed slightly from the waist.

I looked at him and then at the watch. "I don't know what to say."

"'Thank you' would be the usual response."

"Thank you!"

"It looks good on you. I think my father would approve. Now, just keep it safe."

"I have been ... I will."

"I know you will. Now, back to breakfast."

He took a fork and started to dole out the pancakes, beginning with Megan.

"Not too many for me," Mom protested. "I've been trying to watch my carbs."

"A couple of extra pancakes won't hurt you," he said as he plopped down a stack of six or seven onto her plate.

"And you?" he asked me. "Are you on a special diet, too?"

"Yeah, I'm on a see-food diet. I see food and I eat it."

"That's a diet I can live with!"

He forked out a stack of pancakes for me that had to be ten high, and then put an equally tall pile on his own plate.

"The lilacs are lovely," my mother said. "Where did you get them from?"

"There's a beautiful lilac bush over on the other side of the base. I sort of liberated them when I was out."

"You must have been up really early," I noted.

"Not up early so much as not getting to sleep at all," my father said.

"Not at all?" I questioned.

"I went to bed beside your mother, but once she'd drifted off I realized I wasn't anywhere near sleepy. I'm still on Kandahar time."

"I didn't even realize you were gone until I woke up this morning," my mother said. "I didn't hear you get up."

"I tend to move quietly," he said, in an understated way.

He actually moved like a cat. Somehow the floorboards that creaked under my sister's weight remained silent when he moved over them—at least when he wanted them to stay silent. He might have been stomping around the house earlier, but when he was in soldier mode he could move around the house as if he were invisible, like some sort of ninja. That was all part of his training. For such a big man, he could move so silently that you wouldn't even hear him coming. You'd be working on the computer, look up, and jump because he'd be standing right overtop of you.

"Sleep is overrated," he said. "I've gotten so used to being on duty for days at a time that I've learned to grab sleep in little bursts."

"You could take a nap this afternoon," my mother said.

"I *could,* but I was thinking that if I stay up all day instead, then maybe I could get myself synchronized with the time here."

"But you should consider a nap," my mother insisted.

"I will if I'm tired. It's just that I feel so awake. Maybe it's the excitement of being home."

I tried to figure how this could be anything close to excitement compared to where he'd been and what he'd been doing.

"When I knew for sure I wouldn't sleep I decided to go for a run."

"In the middle of the night?" I asked.

"Why not? It's cool and quiet. Besides, it felt really good to be someplace where I knew that nobody was going to try to . . ." He paused. "To be someplace that was so familiar. So, how did the rest of you sleep?"

"Like I said, so solidly that I didn't know you were gone," my mother said.

"Me too," Megan agreed.

"And you slept the whole night in your own bed," my mother added.

"I like my bed," she said.

"And I *love* your pillow," my father said. "I never dreamed my daughter was such a great artist."

"Do you really think it's good?" Megan asked.

"Not good. Great. Maybe they should have sent the pillow to Afghanistan and I could have stayed right here. And you, Marcus?" he asked.

"Me? Me what?"

"How did you sleep?"

"Not too—"

My sister knocked over her glass and the orange juice spilled across the table.

"Megan, you should be more careful!" my mother scolded.

"Sorry! It was an accident!" Megan grabbed the now-empty glass and righted it.

"Of course it was an accident," my father said. He reached out and grabbed a fistful of napkins and started to sop up the juice.

"Thank goodness the glass didn't smash," my mother said. "That's why we should only use the good dishes and glasses for special—"

She stopped herself, and I could tell by her expression that she realized that she was not only criticizing my father for putting them out, but also suggesting that today wasn't special.

"—which is why I'm so happy that your father put them out this morning, because this is *such* a special occasion."

Nice catch, Mom.

"I'm glad you agree," my father said. "But, to be honest, every time we sit down together as a family it's a special occasion."

"That's sweet," my mother said.

"No, no, really, I'm serious," he said, nodding his head enthusiastically. "So what's the point in putting things away, locking them up for special occasions that might not happen? Why not use them, enjoy them? And if something breaks," he shrugged, "it breaks. It's just a bunch of glass and pottery."

"But these plates are from our wedding and—"

"I know they're special," my father said, cutting her off. "And if you want them never to be used again, that's fine, too."

"Not never, I *love* these dishes," she said.

"Then we'll put them away and only use them when you want. It doesn't matter to me if we use paper plates. All that matters is that we're here, together, safe, sharing a meal. What could be better than—?"

The phone rang and my father jumped to his feet, banging the table with his leg and causing the dishes to rattle. My sister shrieked with shock. I reached out and grabbed my glass before it could topple over.

My father was standing, his hands out, fingers locked in fists, crouched over, his face twisted in an expression of shock and scary seriousness. The phone rang again.

"It's the phone," he said, and he relaxed. "It's just the phone ringing."

"Of course it's the phone," my mother said.

"It surprised me," he said. "It's really loud."

"I'll get it," my mother said.

"No, I'll get it," my father said. His expression changed to a big, broad smile. "After all, I'm already up."

CHAPTER FOURTEEN

"I COULD TAKE the bus," I said.

"Of course you could," my father said, "but I'm here, so I'll drive you. Grab your backpack."

I wasn't going to argue. A drive would be nice. And a drive with my father would be even nicer. All through breakfast I'd found myself staring at him. I noticed my mother and sister were doing the same. Like as long as we kept our eyes on him he couldn't disappear. But if we looked away or blinked ... well, who knew?

Dad gave my mother a kiss and a big hug and then did the same with Megan, sweeping her up in his arms. He tried to put her down, but she held on and wouldn't let him. Finally he handed her over to Mom.

"I'll be back in an hour or so. I want to pick up a few things from the hardware store." He gestured toward the sink. "Doesn't that dripping drive people crazy?"

"A little bit," I admitted.

"It's also wasting water," he added.

I gave him a questioning look. "It's just a few drips."

"A few drips add up. Where I came from, people would practically—" He stopped mid-sentence. "People would really value even small amounts of water." He turned to my mother. "And could you do me a favour and make sure the leftover pancakes are wrapped up, and could you save the batter I didn't use?"

"Sure, of course," she said.

"I could use the batter to make more pancakes tomorrow, or even the day after … we could warm up the leftovers first … I don't want them to go to waste."

"Of course," my mother said. "I'll take care of it."

He reached over and gave her another kiss. That was sort of nice and sort of embarrassing. PDAs when they involved your parents were a little much. At least nobody else was around to see it happen.

My father scooped up the car keys and I grabbed my backpack. We left the house and climbed into the car.

"Did you notice the bumper sticker?" he asked.

"Bumper sticker? What bumper sticker?" Obviously not.

"I brought it with me and put it on last night. Go take a look."

I got out and circled to the back. There it was: *"If you don't want to stand behind our troops, feel free to stand in front of them."*

"What do you think?" he yelled out his window.

"Pretty good!" I ran around and quickly climbed back in.

"Won't be long before I'm in the passenger seat and you're driving," he said.

"Not long. I can't wait."

"Me neither. I always wanted a chauffeur."

He started the car and it rumbled noisily.

"Jeeze, it sounds like a tank!"

"It's the muffler, it's going."

"Sounds like it's already gone. Might not be the muffler, though. Sounds more like the exhaust pipe. I'll have a look at it when I get back."

"That would be good," I said.

"It would be. No sense in people being able to hear us coming. It's better if we can move as silently as ..." He let the sentence trail off. "I sort of forgot where I was. Got to fix it, anyway."

He backed out of the driveway. We drove down the street, turned the corner, the next corner, and we were on Courtney's street. He slowed down as we passed her house.

"Your mom told me about you taking care of the O'Hearns' house," he said.

"Seemed like the least I could do."

"Looks like the lawn could use a cut," he said.

"I'll do that when I get home after school."

"Tell you what, how about if I do it?"

"That's okay, I can take care of it."

"No, let me. It's at least something I can do for them. He was a pretty decent guy."

We kept driving.

"When is the family coming back?" he asked.

"Courtney thought it would be before this, but her mother's having a hard time. She thinks maybe next week."

"Terrible thing," my father said. "Just terrible."

Call me selfish, but at that point I really didn't want to think about what Courtney was going through— I just wanted to be happy with my dad, and not feel guilty for having a father when she'd lost hers. Still, I *did* feel guilty.

We stopped at the gate to the base and waited for a car to pass.

"There should be sentries stationed at the guardhouse checking vehicles," my father said.

"I was thinking the same thing."

"As it stands now, anybody could wander onto the base at any time and do whatever they—"

Again he stopped himself mid-sentence. He'd been doing that a lot. Thoughts would race into his head and then he'd think better of finishing the sentence and stop himself. He was really talkative and the words seemed to be rushing out. It was like he hadn't spoken to us for nine months and now he was trying to make up for lost words and lost time.

"I think we all have to go to Cyprus," my father said.

My father and the other returning soldiers had spent three days at a NATO facility so they could "decompress" after being in combat. That was standard practice. Partially it was to debrief them about their mission, but it was also to give them a transition between being at war and being home.

"It's one of the most beautiful countries in the world."

"Sounds as though you really liked it."

"I loved it! Although maybe it had more to do with where I'd just come from than where I was. You have no idea how wonderful it is to walk around a place knowing that nobody is trying to ..." Again he stopped in the middle of his sentence.

"With nobody trying to kill you," I said, completing what I guessed he was going to say.

"Yeah, with nobody trying to kill you. Like now, I'm driving down the road and I don't have to worry about being blown up ... actually, with all the noise this car is making it sounds like it *has* been blown up. I gotta tell you, this car makes me feel a little uneasy."

"The muffler isn't that bad."

"It isn't the noise, it's all this glass."

"The windows?"

"The windows, the windshield, the back. I feel way too exposed. And the whole car is so tinny, well, at least compared to what I'm used to driving."

"G-Wagons or Coyotes?" I asked, referring to the two most common vehicles.

"Coyotes. G-Wagons aren't much better than this."

"Come on, they're a lot more solid than this car."

"More solid, but neither the car nor the G-Wagon is going to survive a direct hit. Either one, you'd be dead. Here, at least, with all the glass I guess I'd have a better chance of seeing it coming."

We drove along and he started to whistle, sort of an off-key accompaniment to the muffler.

I noticed that as we were talking we had started to drift farther and farther out of our lane until we were almost straddling the yellow line in the middle of the road. Up ahead, in the distance, there was a pickup truck coming toward us. I eyed it a bit nervously.

"You know," he said, "the Afghans I met are really not that different from us. Maybe they speak another language and have different customs ..."

The truck was getting closer. "Dad."

"... but they still feel the same love for family and grieve deeply when there's a death."

"Dad! There's a—!"

The truck honked and my dad swerved back into our lane. The truck's horn kept blaring as it passed by us.

"I saw you, buddy," he said. "No need to be rude."

"You were over the line," I pointed out.

"Yeah, I realized that, just a habit."

"I don't understand."

"In Afghanistan you always drive in the centre of the road. You want to keep as far away from the sides as possible because that's where the bombs are planted."

"No bombs here."

"Good thing, too," he said. "Wouldn't want to be hit in something this flimsy. You want to be in a Coyote."

"What was Captain O'Hearn in?"

"A Coyote."

"But you just said—"

"It's solid, not indestructible. You hit a big enough bomb and it would kill you if you were in a tank. At least he went fast. Probably didn't even know what hit him. Sitting there one second, probably talking to his buddies, and then bang, it's over." He paused and shook his head slowly. "He shouldn't have even been there."

"In Afghanistan?"

"Outside the wire. That's no place for admin people to be."

"Then why was he?" I asked.

"He was headed to one of the outer bases to try to fix their supply problems. He didn't even need to go."

"He didn't?"

He shook his head.

"Then why ...?"

"Bragging rights ... being able to tell everybody that he was up country. At least he went quick. Look, you can't be talking to anybody about this—especially his daughter.

"I wouldn't talk to anybody about anything you tell me."

"I know," he said. "I just needed to say it."

I'd noticed that he was drifting back over the yellow line again.

"We used to talk about it. That's how we all want to go. No time to regret, no worry for the rest of your platoon. You're there and then you're gone. That's what a sniper aims for when he shoots. You want the person to be dead before he even knows what hit him, dead so fast he doesn't even twitch his trigger finger. Clean. A good kill."

"Did you . . . ?" I stopped myself two words into the question I knew I shouldn't ask.

"Did I kill anybody?" he asked, turning partway toward me.

"You don't have to answer."

"I don't *have* to answer. You know all those competitions I've won?"

"Of course." There was a row of trophies and a wall of certificates. My father was an amazing marksman.

"They sent me over there to do a job. I did my job," he said. His voice was quiet and calm and measured.

We continued to drive, but now there was no conversation. I felt almost grateful that the muffler was so loud. It wasn't that much farther to school.

The car started to drift over the line again. "Dad."

He turned to me and we drifted even farther.

"The line. You're over the line again."

"Oh, sorry. It's going to take a while for me to adjust," he said. "Maybe it would be safer if you were the driver instead of me."

"Pull over. I'm more than willing to drive."

"Better not. Your mother would kill me. Forget the Taliban. Her I'm *really* afraid of."

My father smiled and laughed, and I laughed along with him.

Funny, all the time he was gone I'd wanted to hear more about what it was like for him, what he was doing. Now, today, I thought I'd heard enough for a while.

CHAPTER FIFTEEN

CAREFULLY, QUIETLY, I moved through the house. I knew I was allowed in, that it was okay for me to be there, but I still felt like an intruder. Courtney and her mother were coming back the next day, and I wanted to make one more pass through the house to make sure everything was all right.

I tipped the watering can ever so slightly to water the big plant in the hall. It was the only plant that always seemed to be dry—it really sucked back the water. The others would be okay, but I needed to check to make sure. Finding a plant dead would be so … so wrong.

I walked into Courtney's parents' bedroom—her *mother's* bedroom. The bed was as she'd left it, unmade. On more than one occasion I'd been tempted to straighten the covers, but I didn't. I wondered which side of the bed he'd slept on. That was such a bizarre thought, but I just wondered. My father always slept on the side by the door, but when he was gone my mother slept there and Megan took my mother's side.

Funny how people take up spaces that belong to other people—like me taking my father's spot at the kitchen table. At first, after he came home, I'd gone on sitting there out of habit, but now my dad was *insisting* that I sit there, while he took my old place. He seemed to like the new arrangement. I wasn't sure, but I thought it had something to do with the wall. In my old spot, he could sit with his back against the wall. He'd just sit there, watching, confident that nobody could come up behind him.

On more than one occasion I'd watched him watching. He'd be doing something ordinary, like bringing in the newspaper, and he'd stand stock-still, moving nothing but his eyes, slowly scanning the scene. Then he'd turn his head ever so slightly and do the same thing again. I guess that was the way it was done in Afghanistan when you were on patrol. It didn't seem so necessary here at home when you were cutting the grass. But, of course, it had to be an incredible transition. One day you're a warrior, watching the world like your life depends on it, because it does, and practically the next day you're at home mowing the lawn. And your biggest worry is crabgrass.

The closet door in the bedroom had been open and remained open. I tried hard not to change or move anything. Inside the closet, most of the space was occupied by Courtney's mother's clothing. But there were a few items that were her father's. Dress shirts and some pants, and there was a full, pressed formal dress uniform—his mess kit—hanging on the inside of the door. On the floor were shoes, mostly hers, but some unmistakably his. What would happen to his clothes? What would happen to his shoes?

There was one more plant to water, the one in Courtney's room. I stopped at the door and inhaled. It was fainter after two weeks, but it still had Courtney's scent … well, I guess the scent of the perfume she wore. There were a couple of times when I was tempted to ask her what it was, but it was just too stupid to tell a girl that you liked the way she smelled. Even though I *did* like the way she smelled.

I stood there in her room. I'd never been in her room before this started. Now I could come anytime I wanted. At least until tomorrow.

We'd talked the night before. She hadn't let more than two days go by without at least checking in with me. Her mother was doing better but was having a hard time coming back to the house. Courtney just wanted to come home.

I watered the little plant on her dresser and looked around the room. Her bed was made, with even the little pillows and stuffed animals neatly arranged. Her entire room was tidy. The door to her closet and all the drawers of her dresser were closed. The books on the shelf were organized alphabetically, and the little figurines and soccer trophies were carefully sorted by year. Courtney was a pretty good soccer player.

I took a deep breath. One more lungful of her scent, and then I left and went downstairs.

I'd carefully stacked the newspapers and the mail on the kitchen table. A lot of it was junk mail and bills, but there were also lots of envelopes that had handwritten addresses. Some had no address or stamp whatsoever; those had been dropped off. I guessed that they were mostly sympathy cards. It would be nice to know that people cared, but at the same time incredibly hard to go through them right away.

I pulled the back door closed tightly and circled around the house. The front lawn and the hedges were all neatly cut and the flower beds tended to. That was mostly my father. He'd been over a couple of times. It was nice of him to come over and do it.

Courtney's house was also probably the farthest he'd been from home since the morning he'd driven me to school and gone to the hardware store. He hadn't even been in the car since then, except for fixing the muffler—actually, the exhaust, as he'd guessed. The noise had been caused by a hole in the tailpipe, and he'd taken a piece of aluminum duct, cut it open along the seam, wrapped it around the tailpipe, and riveted it in place. It worked like a charm. Since then, even when he'd needed something in town—like a washer for the sink or some nails for the back fence or paint for the kitchen—he'd sent Mom. After having driven with him, I thought it wasn't a bad idea to keep him off the road a little bit longer.

So mainly he puttered around the house, trying to fix things. He told us that he was so glad to be home that he didn't want to leave his front yard again. He said that back in Afghanistan he didn't daydream about going shopping or out to a movie or out for a drive. All he thought about was being home, and now that he was here he wasn't in any rush to leave it.

Aside from helping at the O'Hearns', the only other time he left the property was to go for a run, but that was more rumour than fact. He apparently went running in the middle of the night. The day before, I'd come down in the morning to find him in the basement, soaked with sweat, doing a workout. He told me he needed to "stay sharp."

He also had one morning when he had to get into uniform and report for duty. They called it *clearing in* and it was basically a formality, letting your C.O. know that you were available if needed.

He was also down in the basement a lot. It was cool and quiet there, and he seemed to really like the little couch in the corner. He still wasn't sleeping much at night, but he did like to take short power-naps, like he'd done in Afghanistan. Twenty or thirty minutes, and he'd be full of energy and ready to go.

Asleep one minute, and then up and talking at lightning speed the next, laughing, joking around like he didn't have a care in the world. And, I guess, compared to what he'd been through, what he'd seen, he didn't. It was really nice how small things that used to bother him didn't seem to bother him any more. A dropped dish, an out-of-place burp that was too loud, a shirt that wasn't tucked in properly—he either didn't notice or didn't care. Really, what were any of those after you'd faced down death—and won?

I still wanted to know more about what he had seen, but I figured he'd tell me in time, when we were both ready. At some point he would quit stopping himself mid-sentence and tell me what he was really thinking.

I knew in some ways his mind was really over there. There were those times when he'd be super-talkative, but other times he wouldn't talk at all, he'd just sort of stare into the distance. It had happened once while he was sitting at the dinner table, and once when we were over at the O'Hearns' doing the outside work. He sort of froze there, holding the hedge clippers. I don't know how long he'd been like that before I noticed, but it was another thirty seconds before he broke out of his trance and started clipping again.

The place he seemed most like himself was in the basement. He liked the cool, but I think he also liked it because it was quiet, and quiet was important. He was really bugged by loud noises, like the doorbell or the phone. In fact he'd made us turn off the ringer on all the phones except the one in the kitchen, and that one was turned down so low that you couldn't hear it unless you were in the room.

My mom said we had to give him space. I understood. After nine months away, three days in Cyprus wasn't enough time to make the adjustment to coming home. He still wasn't even in the same time zone or sleep cycles as the rest of us. It would happen. In the meantime, we'd all just have to be patient.

I walked back to our house. The car was gone, so Mom had to be someplace. I wondered if she'd taken Megan with her. The outside of our house was looking sharp. Dad had stained the porch and sanded and repainted the front door. The grass was, of course, cut, and the flower beds, which had gotten a little out of control, were weeded and neatly edged.

I walked into the house and stopped myself from yelling out a greeting. I assumed my father was home. If he was sleeping I didn't want to wake him, and I tried to remember that he was sensitive to loud noises. So I came in as silently as I could. He'd most likely be in one of two places—in the basement or sitting in front of the computer in the den.

I listened, and then I could hear him—singing softly to himself. He was awake and happy. I followed the voice. It sounded as though it was coming from the dining room. I peeked around the corner.

Dad was standing on a chair, stretching up, putting pink and white streamers on the ceiling for Megan's party the next day. The whole ceiling was covered with streamers and there was a big "HAPPY BIRTHDAY" sign that he'd made strung across the wall. Megan was really excited about her long-delayed birthday party, and I could tell that my father was pretty excited, too.

"Looking good," I said.

My father jumped from the chair, kicking it over, landing on his feet. And then he leaped halfway across the room toward me. I was shocked. His face was a mask of terror. He looked like he'd seen a ghost.

"Don't you *ever* sneak up on me like that again!" he screamed.

He took a few more steps toward me. His hands were clenched into fists, his face white as a sheet. He looked so angry, so serious, that I felt my heart jump up into my throat and I stumbled backwards a step.

His whole body shook violently. Then suddenly he slumped onto the couch.

Slowly I crept forward. "Dad ... are you ... are you ...?"

He looked up at me and shuddered once more. "I'm okay," he puffed out.

He motioned for me to come over, and I did. He took my hand and eased me onto the couch beside him.

"I'm sorry if I scared you," he said, his voice catching over the last word.

"I'm sorry if *I* scared *you.*"

"You just surprised me. I didn't hear you come in."

"I was trying to be quiet in case you were sleeping."

He laughed. A nervous laugh. "I guess I should thank you for being considerate." He laughed again.

I could feel him still shaking, his leg pressed against mine. I swear I could feel his heart pumping, racing, and there was sweat trickling down his face.

"They told us to expect things like this to happen," he said.

"They?"

"The officers in charge of our debriefing. They said to expect, to expect ... what did they call them? Exaggerated startle responses ... that's it." He smiled. "That was certainly an exaggerated startle response, wouldn't you say?"

"I guess so. If I'd known, I wouldn't have come in that way. I'm really sorry."

"Not your fault."

"Are there other things I should know about?" I asked.

"There are lots of possibilities."

"And are you going to tell me about them?"

"No sense in worrying you over things that mostly aren't going to happen. I'm fine."

I wanted to tell him he wasn't so fine thirty seconds ago, but I couldn't do that. He was my father and he was a soldier and he was a hero, and it wasn't my place to contradict him.

"So, what do you think of the decorations so far?" he asked.

"They're very nice."

"Your mom and Megan have gone into town to pick up paper plates and some more decorations and the cake ... enough cake to feed twenty little girls."

"Actually, twelve little girls and eight little boys," I explained.

"Little boys? When did little boys stop being *yucky?*"

"A few months ago," I said. "She thinks boys are less yucky, especially one named Billy."

"Billy? What's his last name?"

"O'Shea."

"Is that Sergeant O'Shea's kid?"

"I think so."

"Good. It's always nice when you can pull rank on somebody's old man if needed."

"Are you going to be okay with the noise that twenty ten-year-olds are going to be making?" I asked.

"I'll put in earplugs."

"Because if you wanted, you could leave, and Mom and I could take care of everything."

"Megan didn't put off her party just to have me leave," he explained. "Besides, if thousands of Taliban can't make me leave Afghanistan, do you really think twenty kids can make me leave my own house?"

He laughed, but *this* laugh sounded like him again. His facial colour was also back to normal and there was no more shaking.

"Now help your old man to his feet."

I got up and took his arm and pulled him up.

"You know, with my training there's no way in the world that you ever should have been able to sneak up on me like that. I let my guard down."

"Cut yourself some slack. You were putting up party decorations."

"It doesn't matter. Letting your guard down is what gets people killed."

"Yeah, but not while putting up party decorations."

"Over there, people die waiting in line for food, sitting at the table for a meal, praying, taking a crap, standing beside your truck, going to a—"

"You're not over there any more, Dad. You're *home*."

"I know that here," he said, touching a finger to the side of his head, "but not necessarily here." He touched his stomach. "Did you notice what I did when I jumped off the chair?"

"I didn't notice much of anything."

"On the way down, as I was leaping, mid-air I reached for my side arm. I tried to get my gun."

"Really?"

"After going nine months with a pistol strapped to my leg it was my instant response, to go for my gun."

"Wow."

"I still feel almost naked without it. Have you noticed that my hand keeps going down to my side? That's what I'm doing, checking for my weapon."

"Maybe, if it would make you feel better, you could wear it around the house," I suggested.

"That would be a terrible idea," he said.

"But if it makes you feel better then—"

"Marcus, you don't understand. If I *had* been wearing a side arm, there's a chance I could have shot you."

A rush of heat ran through my whole body.

"But I wasn't, and I didn't. That's why it's important for us not to have weapons when we're home. I'm just glad I didn't wet my pants."

"Me too," I said, chuckling.

"I'm not joking," he said. "It happens all the time. Soldiers in battle wet their pants."

"Really?"

"Really," he said.

"Did it happen to ...?"

"Only once. Only once."

There was a loud, painful silence. I didn't know what I should say next.

"I still have some decorations to put up before your mom and Megan get back," he said. "Do you think I could enlist your help?"

I saluted. "Whatever you need, sir."

He saluted back.

CHAPTER SIXTEEN

THERE WAS A BURST of thunder and I woke up. The sound of the rain pounding down against the roof and the window was tremendously loud. I looked at the clock on my dresser. It was almost two-thirty. I smiled—the rain might have been pouring down outside but not a drop was hitting my bedroom floor. Another one of Dad's successful projects. There was a crew on the base that was supposed to do all the repairs, but my father said he was tired of waiting for them. Patience wasn't one of his virtues.

He'd spent the better part of two days on the roof replacing shingles and putting down tar and sealing up cracks and chinks. There was definitely an upside to his not wanting to leave the house.

Another burst of lightning—and when the flash lit up my room I saw a figure standing in my doorway!

"Dad?" I said anxiously.

"Yeah, I'm here," he answered softly. "Sorry if I woke you."

"Not you, the storm."

"Yeah, that's what woke me, too," he said. "The thunder."

There was another burst and the room filled with light.

"It's better that it rains tonight," he said. "Wouldn't want it to ruin Megan's party. She's waited long enough."

"Fifteen months is a long time between birthdays," I said. "But on the plus side, now her next one is only nine months away."

"That's the way to look at things. I'd better let you get back to sleep."

"No, that's okay, I'm awake now. I don't think I'll get back to sleep until after the storm."

"Me neither," he said. He came into the room, spun around the chair at the desk to face me, and sat down. "I went down to the basement for a while."

"Probably quieter down there."

"Better, but I was worried so I came up to check on you and your mom and sister."

"Worried about what?"

"Just worried. I had to make sure you were all okay."

"Are Mom and Megan sleeping?"

"Like angels."

"You were asleep before the storm, right?" I asked.

"Sound asleep." He chuckled. "Are you worried about *my* sleep now?"

"I'm worried about everybody's sleep."

"You really did take this 'man of the house' stuff to heart, didn't you?"

"I just tried to help, that's all."

"And I appreciate it. It was reassuring to know that you were here when I was gone, to know that you'd be there for your mother if anything ... well ... you know."

I did know. "Were there close calls?"

He didn't answer.

"You don't have to talk about it if you don't want to," I said.

"It's not that I don't want to," he replied. "I'm just not sure what to say, or I guess, what not to say."

"You can tell me anything," I said.

"No, I can't."

He said that with such conviction that I knew he was right and I was wrong.

"You asked if there were close calls," he said. "But it was worse than that—worse than a few seconds or even minutes of fear or terror or panic. The horrible part was facing the reality that every day there was a good possibility of your worst nightmare coming true. Things could be calm, peaceful, quiet, like a little piece of heaven, and then all hell would break loose without warning. That's the thing, *without warning*."

There was another burst of lightning and I could see my father brace himself so he wouldn't react.

"Big day tomorrow," he said.

"It'll be a great party."

"Yeah, it will be. I wasn't only thinking about that, though. Aren't the O'Hearns coming back tomorrow?"

"Yeah, sometime ... probably towards evening."

"Are you going to go over and see them?" he asked.

"I don't know. I guess I have to wait until Courtney calls me."

"That's smart. You want to support people but you don't want to push yourselves on them. You have to wait until they ask. You have to respect them enough to let it happen on their time. That's something a lot of people don't understand."

The rain seemed to be slowing down.

"You know what the thunder and lightning remind me of?" he asked.

I had a pretty good idea, but I wasn't going to say.

"Artillery. Not just the sound. If you're standing right beside them, the big guns light up when they fire. Funny how sometimes that sound can be terrifying and sometimes reassuring."

"I don't understand."

"When you're out there and you meet an entrenched enemy, you call in an artillery strike. Those first couple of shells, you hope they're going to land where you asked, but you never know. Sometimes they come in short, almost on top of you, so close that the ground shakes and you're hit with clumps of mud. Pretty scary to think you're going to die, but worse because you know it's your own guns, and it would be because of some mistake somebody made—maybe a mistake you made in calling in the coordinates."

"Did that happen to you?"

"Not to me, but it happens. It's hard to hurl a shell twenty kilometres and not miss by a few metres every now and again. But once they're on target, those shells sound like angels singing. You know each one is going to make your job easier, maybe save the lives of your men, or you."

The sound of the rain kept growing fainter and fainter as we talked, sitting close together but hidden by the darkness. It was almost reassuring not to have to look at each other.

"You know, I was there right after it happened."

"You mean after Captain O'Hearn ...? Yeah, you wrote to me about it."

"I was part of what they call the 'extraction team,' the team sent out to get the injured, the dead, the trapped, the pinned down, and the vehicles. We never left anything behind, not even a burned-out vehicle. That's the way it is, no evidence."

"Evidence of what?"

"That they'd gotten one of our vehicles. We didn't want anything they could use as a photo opportunity for propaganda."

"I didn't know that."

"And the Taliban are the same. If they can, they get out all the bodies. Sometimes we'd see where they'd fallen, you know, blood and body parts, but they always tried to reclaim their dead and injured. Got to give them credit for that."

There he was again, saying something about the Taliban that was positive. That always kind of sounded funny to me, even though my father had told me that a smart soldier knew to always respect his enemy.

"That day, they set the trap really well. Blew up the first vehicle in the convoy, the one Captain O'Hearn was in, and it blocked the road and—" He suddenly stopped. "None of this ... *all* of this ... you can never tell anybody ... right?"

"You know I wouldn't."

"Not even your mother."

"Not even her. I promise."

There was silence. Was he going to say anything more or was that the end?

"I'm not sure why I'm even telling you any of this ... maybe because you were the man of the house." He paused. "You did a good job."

"Thanks." I felt a surge of pride that he would say that to me.

"None of this is pretty, but I think I should tell you."

"It'll just be between us."

"I know." He took a deep breath. "Where was I? Oh ... yeah. So the road is blocked, and the rest of our guys couldn't get through, so they had to hunker down behind their vehicles and return fire. It was a real firefight—bullets, rockets, grenades. And of course we were lobbing in artillery shells from a distance. That's what made it so tricky for us."

"I don't understand."

"The regular forces were coming from both ends of the road, but we were coming in cross-country, behind the Taliban positions, so the artillery had to be timed right. They had to keep lobbing shells at them, and lobbing 'em just right, until we were in position."

"And if they aimed them wrong they would have hit you, right?"

"Exactly. So we slipped in behind them, coming in slowly so we could make sure that nobody was behind us."

A chill went up my spine thinking about that.

"I was always up front, the twelve position."

I knew what that meant. Strict military formation. Front man is the twelve, the flanks left and right are nine and three respectively, and the back door, the man pulling up the rear, is the six.

"So we came in slowly, from behind. And they were so worried about the fire from the front and the shells from up above that they didn't even think about us coming. If it hadn't been for the artillery shells, we could have walked right into their positions. We dropped on down behind cover and started counting. There had to be fifty of them, and that was only what I could see, and just on that side. Best guess would have been there were the same number of them firing from cover on the other side of the convoy."

As he was talking I tried to picture the scene in my head. I could see him and his men sneaking up, moving from rock to rock, and finally taking up positions for firing.

"So we calmly started to do our job. It was like a drill, like we're out on the range. We took our positions and we decided which ones were going to be targeted by each of us. We were talking quietly, agreeing on our first hits—no sense in two of us shooting the same target. And then we started firing. They didn't even know what was happening until the first ten or so of them dropped. One after the other.

"And then they knew all hell was breaking loose, and some of them were going to see Allah a lot sooner than they'd planned, but they still didn't know where the fire was coming from. We kept popping them, one after the other after the other."

He paused and let out a big sigh. I could see his silhouette shudder.

"When you're setting up, you have to think of it as no different than being on the rifle range. You find a brace, you target, you control your breath, and then you squeeze off the round. Only there is one big difference. With a target the bullet just enters. With a human skull, it … well, it … it's different, and because it all happens so quickly you're still watching through your scope."

I was grateful for the darkness.

"So that's what happened. We got most of them, but not all of them. Some of them got away. But that was the end of the firefight."

"And then?"

He shrugged. "And then the air ambulances landed and took away the wounded, and the wrecker hauled the burned-out vehicle away, and we all left and went back to base."

"Wow."

"And do you know what one of my strongest memories was of that entire day?"

I was almost afraid to ask, but I had to. "What?"

"We had chicken for dinner that night, and it was probably the best thing I ate my entire time away." He got up from the chair. "It looks like the storm is pretty well ended. See you in the morning."

CHAPTER SEVENTEEN

I BACKED UP QUICKLY against the counter to make way as a gang of ten-year-olds whizzed through the kitchen. They were like some sort of noisy perpetual motion machine. A combination of excitement and massive quantities of sugary drinks and sugary snacks was fuelling the energy level. For a bunch of kids they weren't bad, though, and with the exception of some spilled drinks, muddy footprints, and a broken vase there had been no real damage done.

Supervising a kids' birthday party really wasn't my idea of fun, but I knew Mom needed the help. Besides, I wanted to keep an eye on Dad. I wasn't sure how he'd react to all the activity and noise—especially the noise. I shouldn't have worried. He was acting like another one of the kids, only bigger. And if noise was a problem, he was making the most. He was tossing kids into the air, running through the sprinkler with them, and generally having fun.

He didn't seem any worse for wear for the lack of sleep he got last night because of the storm. I wish I could say the same. After our conversation, I hadn't been able to get back to sleep for hours. I was glad he told me—I guess.

It did make me smile to see him smile. It took me back to when I was Megan's age. He was always the dad who played road hockey with my friends and me, the one who would slump down on the couch with us and watch cartoons. He was also the father who thought up the coolest games. My favourite was Sock Wars.

We'd get a bunch of friends together, then we'd take all the socks out of all the drawers—even the ones in the dirty laundry bin—and roll them into balls. Next we'd divide players and socks into two teams and take up positions. My father would let us turn over chairs and rearrange furniture, whatever we needed to do to make our forts. Then we'd whip the socks at each other. You'd aim for the head. Of course that wasn't easy, and there were many shots that missed the mark—and some that took out lamps and pictures and knickknacks. We'd play that game for hours. My father would never be the first to call it quits. Usually it was my mother calling us for dinner that made us stop.

The phone rang, jolting me out of my thoughts.

"I'll get it!" I screamed, although I wasn't sure anybody could hear me over the noise. I was hoping it was somebody's parent telling us they were coming to pick up their kid.

"Hello!" I yelled into the phone.

There was a pause. "Marcus?"

It was Courtney! "Hi … hello … sorry about the noise."

"It sounds like you're having a party."

Bad timing—I felt really guilty. "Not me. It's my sister. It's her birthday party."

"Oh, that's right. Her birthday was in March but she was waiting until your father got back."

"Yeah." Now I felt even worse.

"How are things going?"

"Pretty good, I guess, you know, for a kids' party."

"I wanted to let you know that we'll be home late tonight … probably not until ten or eleven."

"The plants are all watered and the mail is on the kitchen table and the grass and hedges are all cut," I said.

"That's so sweet of you."

"Well, my father did the hedges and helped me with the grass."

"Tell him thanks from me and Mom. How's he doing?"

"Okay, good, you know, he's fine."

"It's hard for some people when they come back," she said. "My father had a lot of trouble when he came back the first time."

"The first time?"

"Yeah, this was his second trip over to Kandahar. He was there two years ago, too, before your family moved to the base."

"I didn't know."

"It took him weeks and weeks before he was able to settle down, you know, sleep through the night and not be so jumpy."

"My father's pretty jumpy still," I admitted. "Loud noises especially."

"It'll take some time ... So, unless we get in earlier than we're supposed to I guess I'll see you tomorrow."

"Yeah, tomorrow."

"And Marcus ... thanks for being there."

"No problem. Bye. See you tomorrow."

The phone went dead.

My father came into the room trailed by seven or eight kids. "Come on, Marcus, time to cut the cake."

We all followed him back into the dining room, where everybody else was already sitting in a big circle around the dining-room table. Megan sat at the head, with a party hat on her head and a big smile on her face. My father stood beside me at the other end of the table. He gave me a little nudge.

"Pretty nice, huh?"

"Real nice."

Mom came into the room carrying the birthday cake, candles blazing.

"*Happy birthday to you* ..." she sang out, and everybody in the room joined in.

Megan's smile got bigger and bigger as my mother placed the cake in front of her and the song ended.

"Blow out the candles!" somebody yelled.

"Make a wish, make a wish first!" another kid called out.

Megan looked up at my father and smiled, and I knew she'd already made a wish and it had come true—he was standing right there in front of her eyes.

She took a deep breath and blew and instantly all the candles went out ... except one, which finally flickered and then went out as well. Everybody cheered. I felt relieved. In some bizarre way, Megan's wish and that candle going out had suddenly become incredibly important, as if that candle not going out meant her wish hadn't really come true, that something was still going to happen to him, to take him away from us. Stupid, but stupid thoughts can enter your head in the time it takes for a flickering candle to go out.

My mother took the big knife and began to cut the cake. Each sugary piece was put onto a paper plate and they were passed around the table.

There was a loud pop and a couple of the kids shrieked.

"It's just a balloon!" my mother said, and everybody laughed.

It had startled me, too, and—I glanced over at my father. All of the colour was gone from his face and he looked scared, almost panicky. Slowly he backed away and made a hasty exit from the room. It was just a balloon ... but not to him.

CHAPTER EIGHTEEN

IT WAS ALMOST MIDNIGHT. I wondered if they'd gotten home yet. They hadn't been there at eleven-thirty when I'd checked. I went up to my bedroom and looked out at Courtney's house. There was a light on in her room.

My cellphone buzzed. The ringer was always off now when I was in the house. I caught it as it vibrated its way across my dresser and headed for the edge. I thought I knew who it was, or at least who I hoped it was.

"Hello?"

"Hi, we're home," Courtney said.

"I know."

"You do?"

I suddenly felt very embarrassed, peeking at her house. I wanted to lie, but I couldn't do that.

"I can sort of see part of your house from my house," I said.

"You can?"

"Yeah, from my bedroom."

"I didn't know that. What part can you see?"

Now I felt really embarrassed. "Your bedroom ... from my bedroom window."

"Really. Are you in your room now?"

"Yeah."

"I'm going to go to the window. Tell me if you can see me."

I went to my window. While I couldn't make out details I could see she was definitely there.

"You're waving," I said.

"I am, but I can't see you."

"My lights are out. I'll flick them on and off a few times. Tell me if you can see it."

I went over to the wall and switched the lights on and—

"I can see your room!" she exclaimed. "Come to the window so I can see you."

I went over.

"There you are!" she said.

I gave a little wave.

"Now that I know about this, I'm going to have to be more careful about pulling down my blinds when I get changed."

I didn't know what to say to that! I hadn't known what to expect, but her joking around surprised me.

"You don't have a telescope or a pair of binoculars aimed at my window, do you?"

"Of course not!" I exclaimed. "I'd never do that!"

"Marcus, I'm kidding," she said, and laughed. I liked the sound of her laughter. "Of course … But you'd better keep *your* blinds down. No telling when I might get a pair of binoculars myself."

This time I knew she was joking and I laughed along with her.

"I have a present for you," she said.

"You do?"

"A thank-you for taking care of the house and taking notes for me. Don't expect anything too fancy."

"I wasn't expecting *anything*."

"I can't wait to give it to you … do you want to meet now?"

"I guess that's okay."

"We could meet in our spot."

I knew that she meant the swings in the park. I'd thought about that as being *our spot,* too.

"Is your mother okay with that?" I asked.

"She's sound asleep. She takes sleeping pills every night."

"I guess that's a good idea if she needs them."

"She does. They help. My father was on them when he came home the first time. They helped to get him sleeping right again."

I wondered if that would be good for my father as well, but I didn't really know if I could suggest that to him.

"Are you okay to come out?" she asked.

"No problem," I said. "I'll just tell my father."

"Is he still awake?" she asked.

"Yeah, he hasn't quite gotten off Kandahar time yet." He was downstairs in the den on the computer. "He won't mind."

"Good. I have to get ready a bit. I'll see you there in fifteen minutes, okay?"

"Okay. See you then."

I wondered what she had for me. Was I supposed to have something for her? No, that didn't make sense … although, was there something I could bring her? A piece of cake? No, that made no sense. Better to go empty-handed than with something stupid.

I went downstairs and cut through the dining room to the den. I wanted to move quietly enough so as not to wake people upstairs but noisily enough that my father would hear me coming. By the time I got to the door he had already spun around to face me.

"Can't sleep?" he asked.

"I thought I'd go out for a bit."

"Out? It's after midnight. Where are you going at this hour?"

"To see Courtney," I explained. "She called me."

"Oh … okay … I understand. Just don't be too late."

"I won't be."

His computer pinged—he'd received a message.

"I'm talking to the guys," he said. "On the base."

"In Kandahar, right?"

"Yeah. I check in with them a couple of times a day. Do you know what the temperature is supposed to be there today?"

"Somewhere in the mid-forties?" I said.

"Good guess. Forty-four, and they're expecting a big dust storm. Man, those storms are something else. I have to make sure that we …" He laughed. "I guess *they* have to make sure that *they* hunker down." He got that faraway look in his eyes. "You know, I'm so glad to be home, but sometimes all of this," he said, gesturing around, "seems less real to me than over there. Does that sound crazy?"

"No," I said, although I thought maybe it did.

"I had a feeling you'd get it. You know, you're the only one I talk to about any of this stuff. I don't even talk to your mother about it … I don't know if she would understand."

And I knew he really wasn't talking to me about much, so he must have been saying virtually nothing to Mom.

"I worry about the guys, wonder how they're doing. I guess I even feel a little guilty that I'm not there to help." He paused again. "I know this is my home, but in some ways it feels like I'm visiting here and I live there. That I don't belong here, but I'm needed there. All I can do is keep in touch." He paused. "Even though I know I'm needed here, too."

His computer pinged again and he swivelled his chair to pick up the message. "Why don't you go and see Courtney?" he said. "Tell her hello, and tell her I'm sorry. And don't be too late, okay?"

"I won't be long."

My shoes were waiting in the front hall and I slipped into them and out the door. I didn't want to keep Courtney waiting so I started to jog, but not too quickly. I didn't want to arrive all out of breath and sweaty. I rounded the first corner and then the second, and I could see the park. I saw her right away, or at least her outline. She was sitting on the swing.

As I got closer she stood up and ran to meet me. She threw her arms around me and gave me a big hug. I hugged her back.

"It's so good to see you," she said.

"It's good to see you."

She took me by the hand and led me back to the swings. She sat down on one and I took the one right beside her.

"It feels like I've been gone forever."

"Two weeks is pretty long," I agreed.

"It seems like two years. I bet a lot happened while I was gone."

"Not that much. I took really good notes for you, but other than that, nothing ... well, except for, you know, my father coming home."

"You all must be so happy."

I could only imagine how it must have felt for her to say that, given what she'd been through. Maybe I should have lied, but she'd have seen right through me anyway.

"Really happy," I admitted, feeling more than a bit guilty. "He said to say hello to you," I added, repeating half of his message. "He was still up. He was on the computer."

"Talking to the guys in Kandahar, right?" she said.

"How did you know that?"

"My father did that a lot," she said. "When he couldn't sleep he was on the computer all through the night talking to people over there. Your father is having sleeping problems, right?"

"Sleep is one thing. Loud noises really bother him, too."

"Same with a lot of the guys. I heard where you should never have balloons at a welcome home party because they might—"

"Pop," I said, cutting her off.

"You know about that."

"I didn't, really. I sort of guessed." I didn't want to tell her about my father's reaction. I felt embarrassed for him. "But all those things, your father got over them, right?"

"He did. It took a couple of months."

I could wait a couple of months.

"Well, at least a couple of months after we got into therapy," she said.

"I don't understand."

"We all went, me and him and my mom, a couple of times a week to talk to the base counsellor. And I also did a group."

"Oh, group, okay," I muttered.

"Have you got a problem with group counselling?" she asked.

"Of course not," I lied. "My sister was in one of those groups the whole time my father was away."

"But you weren't?"

"No. I mean, there's nothing wrong with them ... if you need them. It's just that I never needed one, that's all."

"It helped us all," she said. "Are you and your family scheduled to go to see the counsellor?"

"My father mentioned something about having to see somebody, but I don't know about the rest of us ... we might."

"We're going to start seeing the counsellor again," Courtney said.

"That's good."

"Good for me, but not for you?" she asked.

"Yeah, well, my father didn't—" I stopped myself before finishing the sentence but I knew she could finish the thought. What a stupid, *stupid* thing to say.

"Here ... this is for you," Courtney said, breaking the awkwardness. She reached out and handed me a little bag.

I pulled out a piece of tissue paper and underneath that was a baseball cap. I pulled it out. It had a big Canadian flag on the front.

"Do you like it?" she asked.

"I love it. Thanks."

"I thought you might. Are you going to try it on?"

"Of course." I put it on, snugging it into place.

"That looks so good. I just hope the brim doesn't get in the way."

"Get in the way of what?"

She got up from her swing and before I could move she reached over, wrapped her arms around my neck, and kissed me. I kissed her back.

She released me. "I guess we got around it. I gotta go."

Before I could even think of what to say or how to react she was gone, running off, leaving me on the swing, in the dark, wearing my new hat.

CHAPTER NINETEEN

"YOU ALMOST READY for school?" my father asked.

I looked up from my breakfast. He was standing there in full combats. I was more than a little thrown. I'd only seen him in uniform once since he got back. He was usually in work clothes or a pair of shorts and sandals.

"Yeah, I'm almost ready for school," I said. "You're in uniform."

"Have to report in today," he explained. "I have an interview."

"With who?"

"MFRC, probably some kind of counsellor."

"What do they want to talk to you about?"

"They need to ask me about my transition back here. How I'm handling things. Nothing serious, just standard operating procedure."

"And what are you going to tell them?"

"That I'm glad to be back."

"Nothing else?" I questioned.

"What else should I tell them?"

I sat there with a gigantic question hanging in the air. I knew there were things he should probably tell them about, but really, I couldn't say any of that to my—

"Look, I know that I'm having some sleep problems," he said. "And let's face it, I'm more than a little embarrassed to tell them that I get jumpy around balloons and lightning." He laughed. "Not exactly the fearless Special Forces soldier, huh? Can't you see the TV ad? A bunch of heavily armed, highly trained soldiers moving into combat, and then a balloon breaks and they all run away screaming, three of them having wet their pants?"

I couldn't help but laugh.

"Not the best recruiting campaign." He changed his voice to sound like a TV spokesperson. "The Canadian Forces—serving with courage, with commitment, with bravery … unless there are balloons."

"The balloon made me jump, too," I said. I don't suppose that made him feel much better.

"I know you're worried, and I appreciate it, I do," he said. "But really, none of that stuff means anything. Think of the people with real problems." He paused. "There are soldiers coming home without legs, with bad burns, head trauma … me, I get spooked by balloons. That could only present a problem if the Taliban start using balloons instead of bombs. Or maybe if I decide to make a career change to birthday party clown!"

He smiled, and I smiled back. Of course what he said made complete sense. It had only been a couple of weeks. He *was* sleeping better. And even if he was having a couple more glasses of wine at night to help him get drowsy, how was that any worse than taking sleeping pills? He was hanging around the house a lot, but who wouldn't after being gone so long? He *was* doing better.

Megan came running into the kitchen. "Daddy, can you—?" She skidded to a stop and then backed up a step. She looked confused ... no, scared.

"What's wrong?" my father asked. "What's wrong, honey?"

"Why are you wearing that?" she said. "Why are you in your uniform?"

"I'm still a soldier."

"But ... but ... you're not ..." Her lip began to quiver like she was going to cry.

My father swept her up in his arms. "I'm not going anywhere," he said, quietly, almost whispering in her ear. "I'm wearing my uniform today because I have to report in. I'll be standing right here when you come home from school today."

"Promise?"

"Pinkie promise."

They hooked pinkie fingers. She snuffled away the tears and broke into a smile.

"Now you'd better get back upstairs and get ready for school."

He gave her a kiss and put her down. She scampered out of the kitchen and back toward her bedroom.

"I didn't mean to worry her," my father said.

"Maybe you could walk her to school," I suggested.

"I was thinking about driving you to school."

"Me?"

"I need a few more things at the hardware store," he said.

"I could get them after school, after rugby. Maybe Mom could pick me up?" I asked. It wasn't just that I was being helpful. I wasn't sure I wanted to drive with him yet.

"No, I was thinking that I haven't been off base for a while and maybe I could drive you to school and then go and get what I need."

I hesitated.

"I even promise to try not to drive down the middle of the road," he said, and smiled.

He obviously knew what I was thinking. What choice did I have?

"Deal."

"I'm going to go online for a few minutes to find out what's happening with my men," he said. He looked up at the clocks on the wall. "That was such a good idea, to put up the two clocks."

"It helped us keep in touch with what you were doing."

"And now it's helping me keep in touch. Don't get me wrong, I'm so glad to be here ... but those men, those guys ... you know how I feel about them."

"I know." There was always a special bond between soldiers, even in times of peace, but in times of war that bond became even closer. I understood. Not that I'd ever been there, but I knew all about the band of brothers that soldiers become when they come under fire.

"Finish your breakfast, get your stuff together, and I'll meet you at the vehicle at the time you'd regularly leave."

"With you driving, I could leave a bit later."

"Negative," he said, shaking his head. "My appointment with medical services is at ten hundred hours so I need to leave early enough to get through with the hardware store and back to base. It's considered a bad sign if you're late for your interview. So don't you be late. See you at the car."

He left the room and I went back to my cereal. Maybe the uniform bothered Megan but for me there was something comforting, something familiar about seeing him in uniform again. There was also something about his attitude that was reassuring. Standing there, he seemed to be more precise, more in control, more ... him. I didn't think there was anybody I looked up to more than him, anybody that I'd want to be more like someday. I felt bad for thinking, even hinting, that he needed to tell anybody anything. He was coming through this the way he was supposed to. Better than he was supposed to. And it was a good sign that he could joke about it, wasn't it?

MY FATHER BACKED THE CAR out of the driveway, slowly, carefully, looking over his shoulder for traffic, pedestrians, whatever. He was being careful, but not too careful. I was painfully aware that, despite my belief that he was coming through this okay, I was still watching him closely—especially his driving.

"Notice the sound of the car?" he asked.

"Not really ... oh, that's right, no roaring muffler."

"No roaring *exhaust,*" he said, correcting me. "The muffler was always good."

"What do you need at the hardware store?" I asked.

"A new kit for the upstairs toilet. Do you have any idea how much water that dripping wastes? And some wood and brackets to make shelves in the basement. It really is disorganized down there. Marcus, isn't that Captain O'Hearn's daughter?"

Courtney was on the sidewalk, heading for the bus.

"Yeah, that's Courtney."

Before I could even think to say anything he pulled the car over to the curb, in front of her. He got out of the car and I instantly undid my seat belt and did the same. What was he doing?

She smiled and waved, but she looked a little uneasy.

"Hello, Courtney," my father said. He held out his hand. "I wanted to stop and offer my condolences."

She took his hand. "Thank you."

"We're all sorry for your loss. Your father was a good man and a good soldier."

"Thank you," she said. "And thanks for helping to take care of the house while we were gone."

He shook his head. "No need for thanks. We're all family, and we all need to pull together when we lose one of our own. I'm assuming you're on your way to catch the bus to go to school?"

"It's my first day back."

"I'm driving into town so I'm taking Marcus in. Would you like a ride?"

"I don't want to put you to any trouble."

"I can't see how that could possibly be any trouble. It would be my pleasure."

"Well, then … thank you," she said.

My father led us back to the car. I offered Courtney the front seat but she shook her head and climbed in the back. I was glad I'd offered her shotgun, but happier she didn't take it. I hated riding in the back.

We drove along until we came to the empty guardhouse.

Again, my father muttered, "This is not good enough. I really think this gate should be manned."

We started driving, and I was happy to note that Dad was staying well within his lane. I figured because he knew it was a problem it wasn't going to be one.

"So," my father said, "how long have you two been dating?"

"We're not dating!" I exclaimed. I looked over the seat at Courtney. She looked as embarrassed and surprised as I did.

"You're not dating?"

"We're just good friends," I stammered. Although, did good friends kiss?

"Oh, I figured with all the phone calls and the meeting last night," he said. "But I guess, really, it makes sense that you *aren't* dating."

"It does?" I asked.

"Sure. Courtney's really pretty, and you told me how nice she is and how smart."

Now I felt even more embarrassed. I *had* told him those things.

"So, I figure," he said, "that she could probably do a whole lot better than dating *you*."

There was a shocked, painful silence. How could he say those things, or ...?

He started to laugh. "This is where at least one of you is supposed to argue with me."

Courtney giggled. "Well, I suppose when you put it that way ..."

"Hey! You guys are killing me!" I said. "Give a man a break, can't you?"

My father was loving this! "Here's my advice, Marcus," he said. "You'd better get a move on and ask her out before someone else does. Isn't there another school dance coming up?"

"A week today, next Friday night," Courtney said.

"So, Marcus?" my father asked.

I couldn't believe he was actually doing this to me—to us! This was probably the most embarrassing thing that had ever happened to me in my entire life.

"I know what might make it easier," Courtney said. "I'll ask *him* out. Marcus, would you go to the next school dance with me?"

I was too stunned to answer.

"Better give her an answer before she smartens up and changes her mind," my father chirped.

"Of course I'll go with you!" I exclaimed. "I *was* going to ask you, honestly. I was waiting for the right moment." I turned to my father. "You know, preferably when I wasn't sitting in the car with my big-mouth father."

"I could leave, but then there'd be nobody old enough to—" He slammed on the brakes and I was rocketed forward, caught by my seat belt as we skidded sideways, kicking up dirt before coming to a stop on the soft shoulder of the road.

"Did you see that?" my father screamed.

I hadn't seen anything.

"That truck … that truck!"

"It ran the stop sign!" Courtney exclaimed.

I looked to the right where she was pointing. A little white pickup truck was zipping down the road. It must have crossed right in front of us.

"If you hadn't stopped it would have—"

"Hit us, or I would have hit him!" my father said, cutting her off. "I saw it coming, and it didn't look like it was going to stop. It would have hit us broadside, T-boned us, killed us. I serve a whole tour in Afghanistan, I drive up and down Ambush Alley a hundred times, and I almost die right here at home!"

"But we're okay … we're fine."

"Yeah, *we're* fine."

He pressed down on the accelerator and our car skidded and swerved as the racing wheels tried to catch gravel and then asphalt. He cranked the wheel and we started off on the side road after the other vehicle.

"Dad, what are you doing?" I demanded.

"That driver is a danger. He could be drunk or on drugs. I can't let him drive away like that."

"We could call the police," I said as I pulled out my cellphone.

"And tell them what? We didn't see the driver and we didn't catch a plate number. All I know is that it's a Toyota."

I peered through the windshield. The pickup was pretty far ahead and was throwing up a shield of dust. "It looks more like a Chevy, I think."

"No, it's a Toyota for sure. So, do you think we should call the police and ask them to pull over all the white Toyota pickups in the area?" he asked sarcastically.

He was gaining on the truck. I leaned over and looked at the speedometer. He was doing slightly over one hundred and twenty kilometres an hour. Too fast for a gravel road. The gap closed quickly. Soon we were close enough to tell that he was right, it was a Toyota. But there was still too much distance and too much dust to see anything else.

"Can you make out the plate at all?" my father asked.

"Maybe, sort of … a bit."

"Not good enough. We have to get closer," my father said.

This was silly. We'd practically have to be on his bumper to do that.

"I can almost read it now," Courtney said. "Just get a little closer. I have a pen and I'll write it on the cover of my book."

Now there was no way I could argue.

I had the sense that the truck now knew we were behind and following, and it was trying to open up the gap we were trying to close. We had to speed up even more to close the distance. I looked at the speedometer one more time—we were just under one-fifty! I wouldn't have guessed the old crate could go that fast.

The numbers and letters of the plate were now visible. My father read them out and Courtney repeated them back as she wrote them down.

"Okay, let's back off and call the police," I said.

"Not yet. We have to be able to identify the driver so he can't claim it wasn't him."

"What?"

"We have to pull up beside him so we can make a positive identification."

"Dad, we're going really fast and the road is narrow and—"

"Look!" Courtney yelled. "A train!"

I looked up. I'd been so focused on the truck that I hadn't been looking any farther. Way up in the distance a big freight train was crossing the side road, blocking the way.

My father eased off the gas and the pickup truck moved farther ahead.

"He does see the train, doesn't he?" I questioned.

"If he doesn't he soon will, one way or another," my father said.

The truck slowed down and came to a stop right in front of the railroad crossing. I could see through the back window that there were two men in the cab, and they turned around to look at us. They both had long hair, were kind of scruffy-looking, probably in their early twenties, and the passenger was smoking.

My father brought our car to a stop behind the pickup, but pulled it in on an angle so that it blocked the entire road and the truck wouldn't be able to get past us. They were trapped with no place to go.

"Got ya," my father said. "You two stay in the car."

"But—"

He climbed out of the car before I could finish my sentence, leaving the door open behind him. He started to walk toward the truck, slowly, shoulders square.

I looked down the tracks. The last car of the train was visible. Whatever was going to happen was going to have to happen soon. But what *was* going to happen? My father had said he wanted to look at the driver so he could identify him to the police ... but there were two of them, and what if they didn't want to be identified?

"Stay here," I said to Courtney, and I started to climb out. She reached over the seat and put a hand on my shoulder to stop me.

"He's outnumbered. I have to go and protect his flank," I explained.

"Be careful." She released her grip and I got out of the car.

My father was approaching the truck and stopped right in front of the driver's door. I started wide to come at it from the passenger side—three o'clock.

"Good morning!" my father yelled so his voice could be heard above the train. His voice was loud but very calm. "I'm assuming you know what you did back there by the highway."

"I didn't do nothing!" the man protested.

"You almost hit my vehicle."

"I saw you coming and I knew I could cut in front of you!"

I moved in slowly. Both of the men were focused on my father and my approach was masked by the thunderous sound of the train pounding by.

Both men were both pretty seedy-looking. They were the sort of people that I'd cross a street to avoid.

"If I hadn't taken evasive measures you would have hit me!" my father yelled. "You almost forced me into the ditch."

"That's your problem!" the man snapped.

"No, it's your problem."

"Look, just because you got yourself a uniform doesn't make you a cop. Why don't you bugger off before—"

My father reached into the truck, grabbed the keys, and yanked them out of the ignition.

"What are you doing?" the man demanded.

"Shouldn't that be obvious even to you?" My father turned and heaved the keys into the field, where they disappeared into the tall grass and weeds.

"You can't do that!" the man screamed.

"I just did."

The last train car passed and my father turned to walk back to our car. The driver opened his door then and started to get out. Before he could, like a leopard, my father leaped back and slammed the door shut so that it banged into him and he hollered in pain. My father reached into the open window again, but this time he grabbed the man by the shirt! He started to pull *him* out through the window!

The passenger tried to grab the feet of the screaming, struggling man, but my father ripped the driver free, taking him completely out through the window. The passenger scrambled and turned to get out, but stopped as he saw me standing right there outside his window. The only way he was getting out was through me.

"Don't even think about it," I said. "You're just the passenger until you get out, and then you're involved."

He nodded his head in agreement. He looked afraid. He slumped back into his seat and stared forward out the windshield, like if he didn't see what was going on he wouldn't have to get involved.

My father had tossed the man aside. He opened the driver's door, reached in, and grabbed a liquor bottle—half empty—from the floor. He opened it and poured the contents on the ground—on the man lying on the ground! He then took the empty bottle and threw it into the field. I heard it smash.

He looked over at me through the cab, through the two open windows. He didn't look surprised or angry to see me out of the car. He nodded. "Let's go," he said, again, his voice completely calm.

We started back toward the truck. I noticed that he was backing toward the truck, not turning his back, and I did the same. That was just smart.

"I'm gonna call the cops!" the man screamed.

"Good, because I'm going to call them, too," my father said. "Impaired driving, reckless endangerment, dangerous driving should be the charges to start with."

We climbed back into the car. My father started it up.

"Please put on your seat belt," he said calmly. He turned to face Courtney. "Is your belt on?"

"Oh, yeah, right." She snapped it on.

Slowly, very deliberately, he did a three-point turn and started back down the side road. I turned around and Courtney put a hand on my shoulder.

"Are you okay?" she asked.

"Yeah, good ... fine." I could feel my heart pounding in my chest.

I looked past her, through the back window. The truck and the two men standing beside it were still visible through the cloud of dust we were leaving. I watched until they were swallowed up by the dust and distance and I couldn't see them any longer.

"Sorry you two had to be here for that," my father said. "Hopefully I still have time to get you to school. I wouldn't want you to be late on account of me."

I looked at my watch—my father's watch, my grandfather's watch. We still had lots and lots of time. Had the watch stopped? I put it to my ear and it was still ticking.

"We have plenty of time," Courtney said. "It's still before eight."

That was the time on my watch, too. It somehow didn't seem possible that it was still so early with all that had just happened, but really, how much time had it taken?

"I'll drop the two of you off and then report the whole incident to the police," my father said. "I guess we're all lucky they were driving a Toyota pickup."

"I don't understand," I said.

"Me neither," Courtney agreed.

"Toyota pickups are what the Taliban often drive, suicide bombers, so I'm always looking for them. If it had been a Chevy or a Ford I might not even have noticed him coming."

He brought the car to a complete stop at the highway, looked both ways, and then turned back on the route we were following, toward the town and school.

"By the way, I thought I told you to stay in the truck."

"I couldn't just let you—"

CHAPTER TWENTY

I GAVE MY FATHER a wave goodbye as he pulled away, leaving us at the curb in front of the school. We'd still beaten the bus by a good twenty minutes, and the place was pretty quiet.

"That certainly wasn't how I expected my first day back to begin," Courtney said.

"I don't think any of us could have seen that one coming. What class do you have first?"

"Math."

We walked up the steps leading to the front door. There was a little more activity inside the school but we were basically alone.

"I can still feel my heart pounding," she said.

"Me too. That was a bit of an adrenalin rush."

"Pretty dangerous."

"Yeah, if that truck had hit us we could have been killed," I agreed.

"Not just that. I mean what your father did. The way he was racing down that road, and then confronting those men."

"What else could he do?" I demanded, defending him.

"He could have kept driving."

"And they would have gotten away."

"Then once he had the licence number he could have called the police."

"He *is* going to call the police."

I felt myself getting more and more angry. How dare she say anything about my father? A guy had to do what he thought was right, and if she didn't like it—

"I'm sorry," she said, putting a hand on my shoulder. "I'm not attacking your father, really."

As quickly as the anger had built, it vanished.

"It's not like it was even his fault," she said.

"No, it wasn't. It was their fault, those two creeps."

"They're the trigger, Marcus, but what your dad did really started in Afghanistan. It's the anger and the adrenalin rush. Road rage is one of the symptoms."

"That wasn't road rage. He was just—"

"He chased a car at high speed and attacked the driver. What else would you call it?"

I opened my mouth, but before I could blurt anything out my head kicked into gear. It *was* road rage. Courtney was right.

"He's seeing a counsellor," I said. "This morning. He has an appointment."

"Well, that's perfect timing. And how about you and your sister and mother?"

"What about us?"

"Are you all going to see somebody, too?"

"Why would *we* need to see anybody?" I was starting to feel angry again.

"For the same reasons my mother and I saw somebody when my dad came back the first time. The same reasons we're going to start seeing somebody again—because we need the support."

"I've been trying to help," I offered meekly.

"And you have helped. I don't even want to think how much harder this would have been without you being there for me. But I need more than that." She reached out and took both my hands and held them in hers. "*You* need more than that ... your whole family does. Sometimes you really need to look at the heavy stuff."

Before I could even think of what to say or how to respond, she pulled me close and gave me a big hug, and I hugged her back.

She put her mouth by my ear. "Promise me you'll talk to somebody."

I wanted to tell her I didn't need to talk to anybody, that I was fine, that my father was fine, that we were all fine.

"I promise," I whispered back.

CHAPTER TWENTY-ONE

I COULDN'T SLEEP—AGAIN. Slowly and quietly I walked past my parents' room. The door was closed and there was no light coming from under the door. They were asleep—well, at least my mother was asleep.

There was some light at the bottom of the stairs. I crept down, again not wanting to wake anybody but also not wanting to be completely silent in case my father didn't hear me coming. I knew exactly where he'd be.

"You in there, Dad?" I called out softly as I crossed through the dining room on my way to the den.

"Yeah, I'm in here."

He was, as I expected, sitting at the computer, eyes glued to the screen.

"Talking to the guys in Kandahar?"

"Got to keep in touch, let 'em know I haven't forgotten them." He turned around to face me. "By the way, I want to thank you for not mentioning to your mother what happened today."

"No problem." When I'd first got home I'd thought about it, but when she didn't ask me, I figured she probably didn't know anything. Better to leave well enough alone, I decided.

"I didn't tell her myself ... didn't want to worry her. You know how she worries."

"That I do."

"It's just that sometimes women don't really understand these things. It was pretty exciting, though."

"No argument there."

"It was the closest I've come to the rush of ... well, being there. And I've got to tell you that I really appreciated the way you backed me up, although you should have obeyed orders and stayed in the car."

"You can't have it both ways, Dad."

"I guess you're right."

My father took a sip from the glass of wine sitting on the computer table beside him. How much had he had to drink?

"I was wondering how things went today with the counsellor."

"Mission accomplished," he said, his eyes once again fixed on the computer screen.

I shook my head. What did that mean?

"I told her that everything was fine, no problems."

"You didn't tell her about anything ... not even what happened with those guys today?"

"Huh! That's the last thing in the world I'd tell her." He took another sip from his glass of wine.

"Are you going to see her again?" I asked.

"Oh, definitely."

That made me feel better.

"I *have* to see her again. We have another appointment in two weeks, and this time I have to bring your mother."

"Mom asked to come?" I asked. That was good.

He shook his head. "They always have spouses come for some sessions. Then I have to go back again a month after that."

"Courtney's father saw somebody when he came back, you know, the first time."

"Everybody has to see somebody ... S.O.P. ... standard operating procedure."

"But the whole family saw a counsellor. He had problems sleeping, and he was really sensitive to loud noises, and—"

"It was different for him."

"It was? How?"

"He wasn't a combat soldier. He wasn't with Special Forces, he was a loggie," my father explained. "If a loggie jumps when he hears a loud noise the worst that can happen is he has to pick up his stapler and his scattered papers." He shrugged. "But for me ... somebody could be killed. If they knew that I was reacting that way they might not think they could trust me with command. They might not even let me go back."

"Go back? What do you mean, go back?"

"Don't worry, I haven't been assigned to return."

"Well, that's a relief!"

"They won't reassign me for at least six months."

"Six months … you could be going back again in six months?" I stammered.

"It could be a year, maybe longer, but eventually I will go back. You knew that, right? That's pretty much a given."

"Courtney's dad went back and that's when he got killed," I pointed out.

"I've got no control over what happens," he said. "All I can do is go and do my duty and take what comes. I can't control fate, all I can do is approach it with honour."

His computer pinged again.

"I guess I should take that. Don't stay up too late."

He turned back toward the computer, leaving me standing there, stunned.

I stumbled out of the room and started up the stairs. I felt like I was walking in a trance. He'd said, "*let me go back* …" Did Mom know about any of this? Here he was, already talking about wanting to go back practically before he'd unpacked from the last trip! It had been the longest, worst nine months of my life, and here he was talking about doing it all over again. Was that fair to any of us? Didn't we have any say in this? And what about what had happened to Captain O'Hearn and his family … was that what was going to happen to him … to us?

CHAPTER TWENTY-TWO

"GOOD MORNING," my mother said as she quietly came into the kitchen.

"Morning."

"Your sister and father are still sleeping. It's good for both of them, but especially your father."

I looked over at her.

"He needs to sleep more. He can't survive on the little sleep he's getting," she said. "I'm not sure how much he slept last night. I was sleeping so soundly I don't even know when he came to bed."

"It was late," I said.

She gave me a questioning look.

"I was talking to him well after midnight, and he was still on the computer when I left to go back to bed."

"He's spending a lot of time on the computer," she said.

She was filling up the sink with water to do the dishes left over from the night before.

"A lot," I agreed. "He's talking to the men in Kandahar."

"His body is here, but in so many ways his mind is still over there," she said, and there was such a note of sadness in her voice that I didn't know what to say.

I was struck by the urge—the *need*—to tell her what had happened yesterday, but I couldn't. I'd sort of promised my father that it would stay between the two of us. Well, really the two of us and Courtney. But what if Courtney mentioned what had happened to her mother, and her mother told my mom? Then she'd be angry that I hadn't told her myself.

"Dad saw the counsellor yesterday."

"I know. He had to fill out a form and answer some questions."

"Do you think he *did* answer the questions?"

"I think he would have tried to give the *right* answers."

"That isn't what I meant," I said.

"I know. I just don't know how to answer you."

"Do you think Dad told the woman anything about the problems he's having?"

She shook her head. "I don't know ... but ... you know soldiers ... proud ... not wanting to admit they need help."

"But you think he needs help, right?"

She didn't answer. The only sound was the dishes banging and rattling in the sink.

I got up from the table and brought my bowl and glass with me. I slipped them into the soapy water.

"Mom, do you think—" I stopped myself ... one side of her face was puffy. "Your face ... what happened?"

"It's nothing," she murmured.

It wasn't *nothing,* and I realized then that she was fighting back tears. The side of her face, beside and above her right eye—the side that had been facing away from me—was swollen.

"What happened? Did you trip or fall or ...?" Then I thought of what else it could be. "Did he hit you?" I asked, my voice barely a whisper.

She didn't answer except to start crying, her shoulders heaving with sobs.

"Did he hit you?" I said loudly.

"Your father would never hit me ... on purpose ... it was an accident."

"An accident? What sort of an accident!" I demanded.

"He was asleep!" she explained.

"He hit you when he was asleep?"

"He has these nightmares," she sobbed. "They're awful ... he's screaming and his arms are flailing and it just happened. When he woke up he didn't even know he'd done it ... it wasn't his fault."

"I feel awful."

I turned around at the sound of my father's voice. He was standing in the doorway.

"You have to know that I'd never do that to your mother, that I'd never hit her … that I never have hit her or you or Megan … you know that, right?"

I did know that. My father had never raised a hand against any of us.

He came over and wrapped his arms around both me and my mother. I could feel the power in his grip. I could also feel him shaking.

"I'm so sorry, Carol, so sorry," he whispered.

"I know that," she answered.

He released his grip and looked me square in the eyes—his eyes were red. It looked as though he'd been crying, too, or maybe he was hung-over.

"Marcus, you know that I would never do anything to harm your mother or you or Megan, that you're the most important things in my life."

"I know that," I said. I also had something else that I needed to say. I took a deep breath. "You need to go and get help, Dad. You need to speak to a counsellor about what's happening."

"I *did* speak to a counsellor."

"You need to tell her what's happening, the problems you're having."

"That's the last thing in the world I'm going to do. Even if I did talk it wouldn't help anything."

"It couldn't hurt."

"Yes, it could," he said defiantly. "You know that." He took his arm completely away from my mother as well, stomped off a few feet, and then spun back around. His expression had changed completely—instead of sad and sorry he looked serious and scary.

"You're too young to understand!" he snapped. "You're a kid. Just because you're wearing my watch and sitting in my seat at the table doesn't mean you're the man of this house!"

"What?"

"I went through this with my old man, too, but I gotta tell you, you aren't man enough to tell *me* what to do. I'm still the father here and you're still the kid, understand?"

What was he talking about? What was he saying?

"Do you really think you're big enough to challenge me?" he demanded.

Before I could answer, he reached out and pushed me, propelling me slightly backwards. I stumbled and tried to regain my balance. My father stepped forward, menacingly. My fingers curled into fists and I stepped forward and—

"Both of you, stop it now!" my mother demanded as she stepped between us. "Just stop it!"

My mother eased my father away a few steps, opening a gap between us. His body seemed to relax slightly but his hands were still in fists and his expression was still angry.

CHAPTER TWENTY-THREE

I SAT ON THE SWING, waiting. The little park was empty now. I'd waited until the last two kids and their mother had left before I'd called Courtney. Now I hoped she'd get here before anybody new showed up. This was going to be hard enough without an audience. I wished it were night instead of day. Some things were easier to say in the dark.

Like magic, Courtney appeared, and despite everything else I smiled. She waved, and I felt myself melt a little bit. She was … she was … well … beautiful. Maybe my father was right—she was too good for me.

She walked right up to me and without hesitation leaned forward and kissed me. I kissed her back.

"So what's so serious?" she said. "You're not trying to get out of taking me to the dance, are you?"

"Of course not."

"Marcus … kidding … what's wrong?"

"I feel bad even talking to you about this."

"You can talk to me about anything," she said.

"It's just that I shouldn't be bothering you with *my* problems. I should be helping you get through *yours.*"

"You have been helping me," she said. She leaned in close. "Let me help you."

I tried not to look into her eyes but she moved so that we locked eyes again.

"Okay?"

"Okay," I said.

"It's your father, isn't it?"

I nodded my head. I needed to talk to her, but it still felt like I was telling secrets, like I was betraying him, betraying my family.

"He went to see the counsellor, but he didn't tell her anything about anything," I said.

"Not even about what happened with the pickup truck?"

I shook my head. "Nothing. My mother doesn't even know about that. He didn't tell her."

"So that means *you* didn't tell her either," she said.

"It just felt like … like … I don't know."

"*I* know. They call it the code of silence."

"What?"

"Everybody stays quiet. They don't want to tell anybody about what they're seeing. And the worst part is that each person has a little piece of the puzzle—they see something wrong, but they don't tell anybody about it so nobody has the whole picture."

I got it. That was like my mother not telling me about the night terrors Dad was having because she didn't want to worry me.

"And it only all makes sense afterwards when everyone sits down later and starts talking at the funeral."

"At the funeral?" I questioned.

"When the person kills himself."

I startled. "What are you talking about? My father would never do that!"

"Lots of soldiers do."

"You don't know my father!" I exclaimed.

I jumped up from the swing and stomped away a few steps, but she followed me, and reached out and took my hand. I fought the urge to break free, and instead I let her turn me around to face her.

"I'm not saying he *is* going to kill himself," she said. "I don't know … I wasn't trying to make you feel bad or say anything—"

"It's okay," I said, cutting her off. "I know you wouldn't say anything to hurt me on purpose."

"It's just that some people *do* kill themselves. Some drink too much, or start doing drugs, or they get violent, they hit their kids or beat their wives. I'm not saying your father, but some soldiers do that."

I was struck, then, by the fact that I hadn't told her about my mother being hit or about my dad pushing me—I was part of the code of silence. I had to make up my mind to either talk, or stop pretending that I really was talking. How ironic—I was talking to Courtney about my father not being honest, but I wasn't being completely honest with her myself.

In a quick burst I explained to her what had happened that morning—what had happened the night before.

"Sounds like classic PTSD," she said.

"What?"

"Post-traumatic stress disorder. It's what happens to soldiers when you put them in combat and they experience terrible things—friends dying, them being afraid they're going to get killed, or having to kill other people—and then how they react when they come back."

"How do you know all this?"

"Remember, I was in group. They told us about stuff like that. We talked about it. Your dad needs to speak to somebody," she said. "All of you do."

"I know ... I just don't know how to make it happen."

"I could give you the name and number of my counsellor and you could talk to her about—"

"I can't do that," I said. "Not yet. Maybe he needs more time."

She took my hands in her hands. "How much time?"

I shook my head. "I don't know. Maybe another week or two."

"And if it gets worse?" she asked. "What then?"

"Then I get that number and make the call."

"Promise?" she asked.

"I already made that promise, remember?"

"Yeah, you did."

"How did you get so smart?" I asked her.

"The only smart thing I did was go for counselling and listen and be honest. That's all."

"I'm so sorry I had to lay this all on you," I said. "You have enough to deal with already."

"We're going to get through it," she said. "What choice do we have?"

I guessed she really didn't expect an answer to that.

"You know what the big difference is between my father and your father?" she asked.

I almost blurted out that her father was dead and mine was alive, but again, I knew she wasn't looking for me to give an answer.

"My father died, so he's a hero. Your father lived, so he's just a survivor, and because he isn't missing a leg or an arm, nobody except you and your mother and maybe your sister can even see the wounds." She paused. "But that doesn't mean they aren't there. That doesn't mean that he isn't wounded."

CHAPTER TWENTY-FOUR

MY MOTHER slowed the car down and pulled it to a stop in front of Courtney's house. There was a light on in the living-room window. I wondered if it had been left on for Courtney or if it meant that her mother was still awake, waiting up for Courtney to get back from the school dance.

"Here we are," my mother said.

"Thank you for the drive," Courtney said.

"It was my pleasure."

There was an awkward pause. Was I supposed to lean over the seat and kiss her goodnight, or get out of the car, or ignore the whole thing or—?

"Why don't you walk Courtney to the door," my mother suggested.

"Good idea."

I could tell that Courtney was relieved, too. We both climbed out of the car. This was better, but now was I supposed to kiss her at the door with my mother sitting there watching us?

My mother leaned over so she could speak to me through the window on the passenger side. "I'm going to go now. I want to check on Megan. So you can just walk home when you're ready, right?"

"Sure, thanks."

The car started off, leaving us standing alone on the sidewalk.

"That was very nice of her," Courtney said.

"She's pretty cool," I said. "Besides, I think she likes you."

"My mother likes you, too."

"Hey, what's not to like?" I questioned.

"Certainly not your humbleness," she joked.

We started up the walk to her house, holding hands.

"I had such a good time at the dance tonight," she said. "For the first time in ages I wasn't thinking about … about anything else."

I knew what she meant. I knew because I hadn't thought about my father for most of the night either. Partly that was because he really *was* doing better. He'd apologized for what he'd said to me, and he was sleeping better, and he had even gone off the base a few more times and nothing weird had happened. Maybe he was right and we'd get through this ourselves.

We stopped at her door.

"Do you want to come in for a while?"

"I really should get home. Besides, I wouldn't want to wake your mother."

"Oh, she's already awake. She's probably staring out one of the windows watching us right now."

"That should make for a great goodnight kiss," I said.

"So, being watched makes you kiss even better than usual? Interesting ... does that make you an exhibitionist? Should we be looking for public displays of affection?" she joked.

"That isn't what I meant to—"

"Just shut up and kiss me."

I gave her a big kiss, and she kissed me back. Then she leaned back and looked into my eyes. "Okay, maybe that *was* a pretty great kiss. Good night, Marcus."

"Good night," I mumbled as she turned, opened the door, and disappeared inside.

I walked down the path and realized that I almost felt as if my feet weren't touching the ground. Somehow, in spite of everything, it was all going to be all right. If I hadn't been afraid someone might see me, I might have skipped all the way home!

Our car was in the driveway and the house was dark. Megan was sure to be in bed by now. Maybe Dad had gone to sleep, too. That would be another good day wrapped up into another good night. I opened the door and heard voices—my mother and father. I followed them into the den. My father was sitting at the computer and my mother was standing overtop of him, her arms around his shoulders. He was crying. I rushed in.

"What's wrong?"

My father looked up, tried to say something, and began to sob.

"There's been a death," my mother said.

"A death? Who, when, where?"

"In Afghanistan," my mother said. "Your father just got word." She gestured to the computer.

"It was one of my men," my father sobbed. "He died … and if I'd been there … if I had been there …" He started to cry even louder.

"It wasn't your fault," my mother told him. "It isn't your fault."

My father got to his feet and stumbled, almost falling over before my mother steadied him. He lurched forward, tripping over his feet again. What was wrong? Was he …? I could smell the alcohol, and there was an empty bottle peeking out from the garbage can. My mother hadn't had anything to drink—she would never have had a drink when she knew she'd be driving—so he must have drunk the entire bottle himself.

"I gotta get outta here," my father mumbled.

"What do you mean?" my mother demanded.

"I gotta get out for a while … clear my head … where are the car keys?" he asked.

"The keys are in my purse, but you can't—"

He brushed by her and staggered past me and out of the room. We trailed out after him, through the dining room and into the kitchen. He had found my mother's purse on the kitchen table and was rummaging through it. He pulled out the keys and dropped the purse back down on the table.

"You're in no condition to drive," my mother said. "Let me."

She reached for the keys and he ripped them away from her.

"I need to get away … I need to be alone."

"But you can't drive!" she protested.

She tried to take the keys again. He pushed her away and she slammed against the wall, banging her head and slumping to the floor!

"Mom!" I ran over. "Are you okay?"

She looked stunned. "You have to … stop him," she stammered.

I turned around. My father was nowhere to be seen.

"You have to stop him."

"You're okay?"

"I'm fine … go … please."

I ran out the door. My father was climbing into the car. I rushed over and leaned in through the open window.

"You can't drive!" I exclaimed.

"I've been driving since before you were born."

"You're drunk."

"I've had a bit of wine, but I'm not drunk."

He put the keys in the ignition and started the car. I remembered what he had done with the pickup truck. I reached in and grabbed the keys, turned off the car, and took them from the ignition. He tried to stop me but his hands slipped off my arm. He reached out and grabbed me by the shirt. I tried to get away but he pulled me forward, and before I could even react he had his hands around my throat!

"Did you think you could get away from me that easily?" he said.

He had me, but I had the keys. I tossed them up the driveway and they landed with a noisy jingle. Instantly he released his grip and pushed me away. I stumbled backwards, falling onto the lawn. The car door opened and whizzed by my leg, almost hitting me, as my father climbed out of the car.

I couldn't let him get to those keys. I scrambled forward on my hands and knees, the pavement biting into my skin. I grabbed the keys and started to move away and—I was flattened, my face crunching into the asphalt. My father was on my back, his full weight pinning me down, forcing the air out of my lungs. He had an arm under my chin, arching me up, holding me in a choke hold. I was completely helpless, unable to move, barely able to breathe.

"You're still just a kid," he said. "I'm the father."

"I'm a kid," I gasped. "But you're not my father."

"What's that supposed to mean?" he demanded.

I tried to gather my breath. "*My* father would never hit my mother."

"That was an accident, I was asleep ... I apologized."

"You weren't asleep tonight!" I snapped. "You're not asleep now when you're hurting me. *My* father wouldn't do that."

His grip tightened around my throat, and then all at once he released me. I turned over and turned around. He was walking down the driveway. The car was there, door open, and the keys were still in my hand. I stood up and watched as he staggered down the street.

I had the keys. He wasn't going to drive.

My mother came out of the house.

"Where's your father?"

"He went. He's walking ... I have the keys." I held them up.

"He shouldn't be out there, not like that. I have to go after him."

I stood up and held on to her arm. "No, you can't go."

"But I have to. He can't be alone when he's like that!"

"I'll go."

CHAPTER TWENTY-FIVE

"HERE." I handed my mother the car keys.

"Your arm," my mother said.

I held it up. The whole forearm was scraped up and bleeding from where I'd been pushed into the pavement.

"You're hurt."

"I'm okay, it's nothing."

I started down the driveway, closing the car door as I passed. I quickly realized that it wasn't just my arm that was hurt. My good pants were ripped, and I felt the sting of ripped skin beneath that, felt my knee begin to stiffen.

"Be careful!" my mother called out after me.

I gave a backwards wave as acknowledgment and picked up my pace. I was going the direction he'd gone but I couldn't see him any longer. He couldn't be far, though; he hadn't been moving very fast. I reached the corner, stopped, and looked. He had to have gone this way, but—no, there he was! He was standing on the sidewalk, partially hidden in the shadows.

I started moving more quickly, jogging. My shoes—my leather dress shoes—weren't made for running, or for silence. He heard me coming and turned. I had a sudden fear that he might start running away. There was no way in the world I could keep up with him ... unless the alcohol had slowed him down. But he just turned around and kept walking.

I got closer and eased up beside him, walking parallel to him and on the road, a few metres away. He looked over at me but didn't say anything. We walked along in silence. I didn't know what to say to him. I didn't even know what I wanted from him. Was I going to try to bring him back home, or let him stay out there, with me keeping an eye on him?

"You're limping," he said.

"Yeah."

"And your arm ... I'm sorry."

"You've been sorry a lot lately!" I snapped.

He didn't answer. Maybe that was too much. He turned another corner and I turned with him in lockstep.

"I ever tell you about Claude?"

"Claude who?"

"Claude Renault. When I was out there on patrol he was my six."

"I don't understand ... oh wait, you mean he was behind you providing cover."

"I'd lead, at twelve, and he'd be right behind me, my six, guarding my back. As long as Claude was there I knew I was covered.

"One time we're on patrol in this village and I'm leading and Claude, he's behind me. He sees this truck coming—a Toyota—barrelling down on me from the side. He yells and I take cover. He opens fire … him and a couple of the other guys. They lay fire on this truck, fill it with a hundred bullets, fill the guy with a dozen holes, and he crashes. The whole truck goes up in a ball of fire … it was a suicide bomber and the truck was filled with explosives. If it wasn't for Claude on my six it would have got me."

"And nobody got hurt?" I asked.

He laughed bitterly. "None of us, but there were casualties. Civilians, maybe twenty injured, five or six killed … at least that's what we figured from the bodies and the body parts."

"Body parts," I mumbled.

He nodded. "Arms, legs, pieces no bigger than my hand. You have no idea how light a kid's arm is until you're holding it in your hand."

I shuddered. Then I suddenly realized why he was talking about this man. "Was it Claude who … who was killed?"

He nodded his head.

I knew what he had to be thinking. "And you wonder, if you'd been there to be his six, would he still be alive?"

He spun around suddenly to face me and I stumbled backwards a half step. "I don't wonder," he said. "I *know.* Because I'm not there, he died. It's my fault, it's my fault!" he screamed. "And that's why I have to go back before anybody else gets killed."

"He didn't die because of—"

He turned away and started to walk again. I hurried after him.

"You know you can't go back right now," I said, trying to reason with him. "You have to wait at least a few months before you do another tour. That's regulations."

"I'm Special Forces. They'll send me back sooner if I request it. I'm going to ask him tonight."

"Tonight?"

"Right now, I'm going to his residence."

I suddenly realized we were on the Commander's street, that I could see his house from where we stood.

"You can't do that!" I exclaimed. I grabbed him by the shirt and spun him around, shocked at how I was able to do that.

He tried to pull away, and then he spun so his arms were holding mine. He was going to try to break my grip, but I wasn't going to let go. He'd have to break my arms to get me to release my grip on his shirt.

"Let go of me or—"

"Or you're going to hit me again? Are you going to put me in another choke hold? Look at my arm, look at my leg—*you* did that!"

His grip on my arms loosened slightly.

"You can't see him now," I said. "Think about it. It's the middle of the night, and you've been drinking. What do you think he'd say? What do you think he'd do?"

His hands slipped off my arms completely, but I still held him, a fistful of shirt clutched tightly in my hands.

"It's more than just tonight. You're not fit to go back."

His eyes flared, but the anger quickly faded.

"You can maybe fool yourself, and you think that you can fool the counsellors, but you can't fool your family. Be honest with yourself. Right now, if you were over there, you couldn't even take care of yourself."

He opened his mouth to say something but no words came out. Instead his jaw began to quiver, and he started to cry once again.

I loosened my grip and then let go of his shirt. He stood there, silent and still.

Slowly he reached down and started to undo the watch that was on his wrist. "I think that maybe you should still be wearing this."

I stopped him. "No, that watch *does* belong to the man of the house … you."

"I don't feel much like a man."

"You're a man I'm proud of as a soldier, proud to have as my father."

"I'm not sure I'm much of either of those right now."

"Maybe not tonight, but I know you're also man enough to admit you need help."

He hesitated, and for a split second I thought he was going to turn away again but he didn't. He looked me square in the eyes.

"You're a good son."

"You're a good father."

He shook his head. "Not tonight."

I hesitated, then, "Maybe not tonight, but you will be again … soon." I paused. "I know they need you over there, but we need you here. Megan … Mom … *me*. We all need you … *all* of you. A good soldier knows when to retreat, when he needs to regroup," I said softly. "Right now, you have to let us take care of you. You have to let *me* be your six. I got you covered."

"I know you do." He put his arm around my shoulders. "Let's go home."

AFTERWORD

WE, AS GRADE 8 STUDENTS, were very fortunate to be asked to read Eric Walters's book *Wounded* and provide him with feedback. We first started learning about global issues in Grade 7 through character education classes. We learned about various historical genocides around the globe, including the Holocaust, Rwanda, Cambodia, and Darfur. We participated in several international video conferences, discussing issues with other schools and a Rwandan genocide survivor.

We extended our studies to the present-day conflict in Afghanistan. We became interested in learning about Afghanistan because many parents from our school have been or are presently deployed there through the Canadian Armed Forces. We began our studies by viewing the CBC documentary *Between Hope and Fear*. This inspired us to begin our own Afghanistan project.

After researching a variety of issues facing the Afghan people of today, including freedom of speech, warlords, land mines, women and children in Afghanistan, health care, the Taliban, and Canada's involvement in Afghanistan, we created our own mini-documentary. During the preparation of our video documentary, we were able to dialogue through e-mails with the Afghan Canadian Community Centre, a school in Kandahar. We found out first-hand answers to some questions that came up during our research.

As students living in a military community, we can all relate to how Marcus, the main character in *Wounded*, would have felt while his dad was serving in Afghanistan. One member of our small group of students, Holly, has a mother who had recently completed a tour in the Canadian military in Kandahar. When her mom was in Afghanistan, Holly was often very confused because she did not know what was going on, so it made her afraid. Every night she would hear on the news about soldiers coming home injured or killed, and she feared that it would be the last time she saw her mom. When her mother finally came home, Holly was very relieved that she didn't have to worry anymore. Through reading *Wounded*, we can more easily identify with how Holly and others must feel while a family member or friend is in Afghanistan. As well, we began to realize that the war doesn't end when they come home to Canada.

We can now appreciate the important roles our Canadian peacekeepers and their families provide, not only to Afghanistan but to other parts of the world. Hopefully this book will enable all of us, including our government, to support our soldiers during their deployment, but especially upon their return.

By the students of
Angus Morrison Elementary School
Caleigh P., Emily P., Chantelle W.,
Jordan B., Jamie M., Holly R., and Andrew M.

AUTHOR'S NOTE

I ALWAYS TRY to experience the realities of my characters. This has led me, among other things, to whitewater rafting, rock climbing, hanging out at a biker bar, walking tigers, running a marathon along the Trans-Canada Highway, and travelling through Kenya. I've often said that I am a "method writer."

For this story, I was able to have the input of people who have served in Afghanistan, children who have had parents serve there, and people who have counselled soldiers and their families upon their return. I offer my thanks for their time and input.

As part of my research I stood on the tarmac at CFB Trenton and waited and watched as a repatriation ceremony took place for one of our fallen soldiers. It was a moving and painful experience. Somehow the story becomes much more than just a story when you can hear the sobbing of those who have lost a loved one.

This soldier was one of over a hundred Canadians who have fallen during our mission in Afghanistan.

They have left behind spouses, sons and daughters, mothers and fathers, sisters and brothers. Each is a hero—not for the ultimate sacrifice they made, but for their willingness to make that sacrifice. We need to remember their deaths, but also remember all those who have served—their brothers and sisters in arms—who are all heroes.

With respect, and thanks,
Eric Walters